MONSUNO®
COMBAT CHAOS™

THE MOTO MUTANTS

Story by
Brian Smith

Art by
Erwin Prasetya

MONSUNO: COMBAT CHAOS
Volume 1
The Moto Mutants

The Moto Mutants
Story by Brian Smith
Art by Erwin Prasetya & Angga Prasetyawan
Cover & Additional Art by Alfa Robbi
Inks by Arum Setiadi & Fandhi Gilang Wijanarko
Colors by Fajar Buana
Letters by Zack Turner

Design/Sam Elzway
Editor/Joel Enos

TM & © 2013 Pacific Animation Partners LLC
"Monsuno" TM & © 2013 JAKKS Pacific, Inc. All Rights Reserved.
Licensed by FremantleMedia Enterprises

Printed in China

Published by VIZ Media, LLC
P.O. Box 77010
San Francisco, CA 94107

10 9 8 7 6 5 4 3 2 1
First printing, June 2013

vizkids
www.vizkids.com

PARENTAL ADVISORY
MONSUNO is rated A and is
suitable for readers of all ages.
ratings.viz.com

VIZ
media
www.viz.com

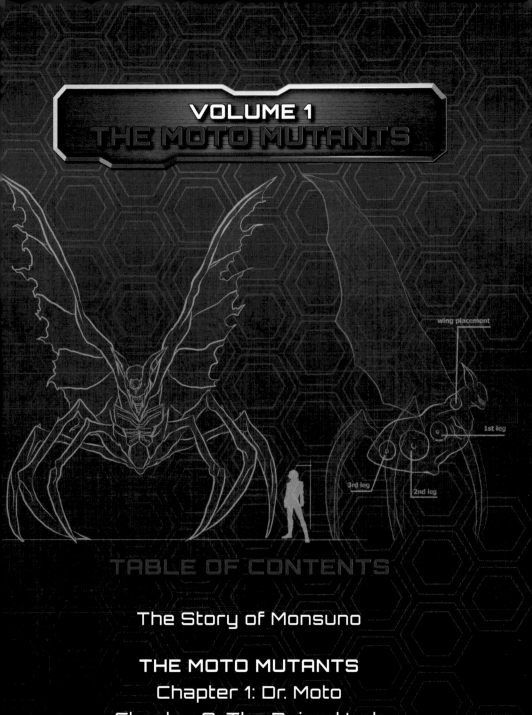

VOLUME 1
THE MOTO MUTANTS

wing placement

1st leg

3rd leg

2nd leg

TABLE OF CONTENTS

The Story of Monsuno

CHARACTERS

CHASE & LOCK

Chase is on a quest to both find his missing father, the scientist who discovered Monsuno, and figure out a way for humans and Monsuno to coexist peacefully. He's learning how to be the hero that he needs to be to make that happen. Chase's Monsuno, the powerful and loyal Lock, was left for him by his father.

BREN & QUICKFORCE

Chase's best friend since childhood. He is a fast-talking genius, but he lacks courage. Bren's loyal Monsuno is the volatile Quickforce.

JINJA & CHARGER

The unpredictable Jinja has no patience for bad guys. She's quick to act and even quicker to tell you if you're wrong! Her Monsuno is the tough-skinned Charger.

BEYAL & GLOWBLADE

Beyal is a mystic monk who would rather meditate than fight. He has a strong spiritual connection to Monsuno that none of his friends have yet developed. Beyal's Monsuno, Glowblade, is a scorpion-like reptile that is always ready to strike at its master's command.

DAX & AIRSWITCH

Dax is the rebel of the team. His act-first-think-later attitude sometimes gets him and his clawed Monsuno, Airswitch, into trouble.

DR. KLIPSE

The main villain in the Monsuno story. He wants to control the world by demolishing society and creating a new world order where he rules with the power of Monsuno. His Monsuno of choice is the terribly scary Backslash.

DR. MOTO

Her secret experiments with Monsuno are about to get out of hand...way out of hand!

HARGRAVE

Dr. Klipse's loyal butler is full of creepy secrets.

THE STORY OF
MONSUNO

65 MILLION YEARS AGO – Meteors fell to Earth carrying life-forms made out of powerful, chaotic, uncontrollable genetic material. This was the Monsuno—origin unknown and the real reason why the dinosaurs became extinct! Soon after, the Monsuno essence fell dormant and stayed that way for millions of years...until...

TODAY – A potent energy source is discovered in the K-layers of the planet. Scientist Jeredy Suno believes he's found a solution to the ever-mounting energy crisis. But what he doesn't know is that this green energy source is a ticking time bomb!

Dr. Suno's research breakthrough could be used to benefit all mankind. But the awakened Monsuno essence could also potentially wipe out humans like it did the dinosaurs!

When Dr. Suno goes missing, his 15-year-old son, Chase, ventures out to find him. Chase discovers the power of Monsuno, and now he and his friends are in an all-out race for survival against dangerous villains seeking power and a secret government agency seeking control of the most powerful creatures ever known...the Monsuno!

THE MOTO MUTANTS

CHAPTER 1
DR. MOTO

Story by Brian Smith

Art by Erwin Prasetya

Letters by Zack Turner

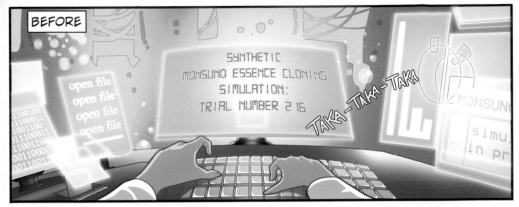

SYNTHETIC MONSUNO ESSENCE CLONING SIMULATION: TRIAL NUMBER 216.

TAKA-TAKA-TAKA

open file
open file
open file
open file

MONSUNO

simul
in pr

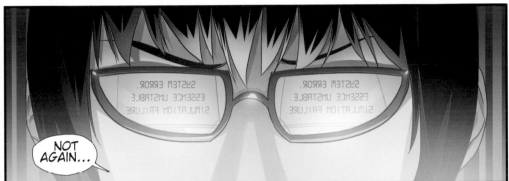

SYSTEM ERROR. ESSENCE UNSTABLE. SIMULATION FAILURE.

NOT AGAIN...

NO! NOT AGAIN!

DR. KLIPSE MAY HAVE DEEMED YOU FAILURES, MY CHILDREN, BUT I KNOW BETTER. YOU ARE ALL BEAUTIFUL... PERFECT...

I WILL MAKE HIM SEE.

SEE WHAT, DR. MOTO?

WHO DARES DISTURB MY WORK...

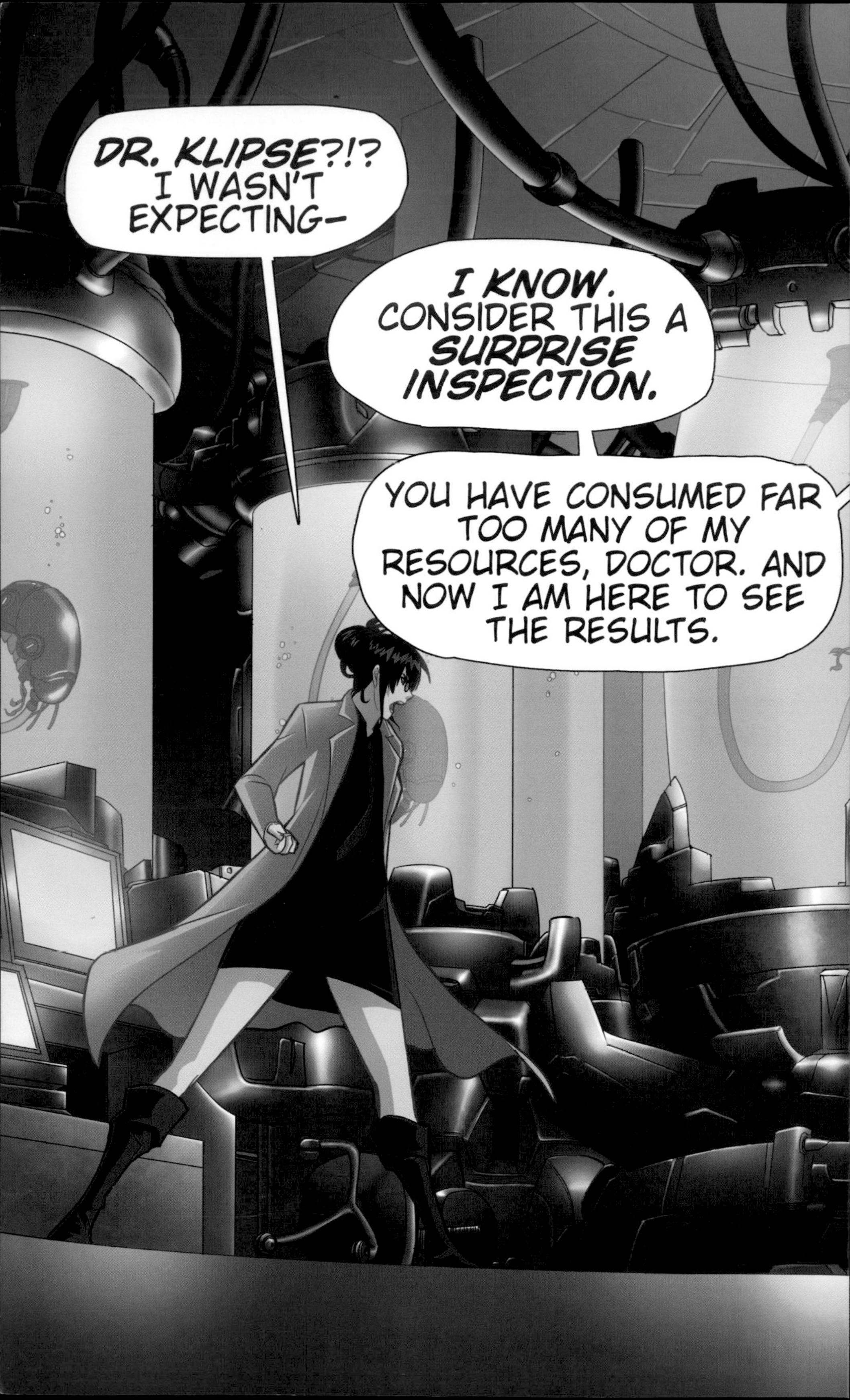
DR. KLIPSE?!? I WASN'T EXPECTING-
I KNOW. CONSIDER THIS A SURPRISE INSPECTION.
YOU HAVE CONSUMED FAR TOO MANY OF MY RESOURCES, DOCTOR. AND NOW I AM HERE TO SEE THE RESULTS.

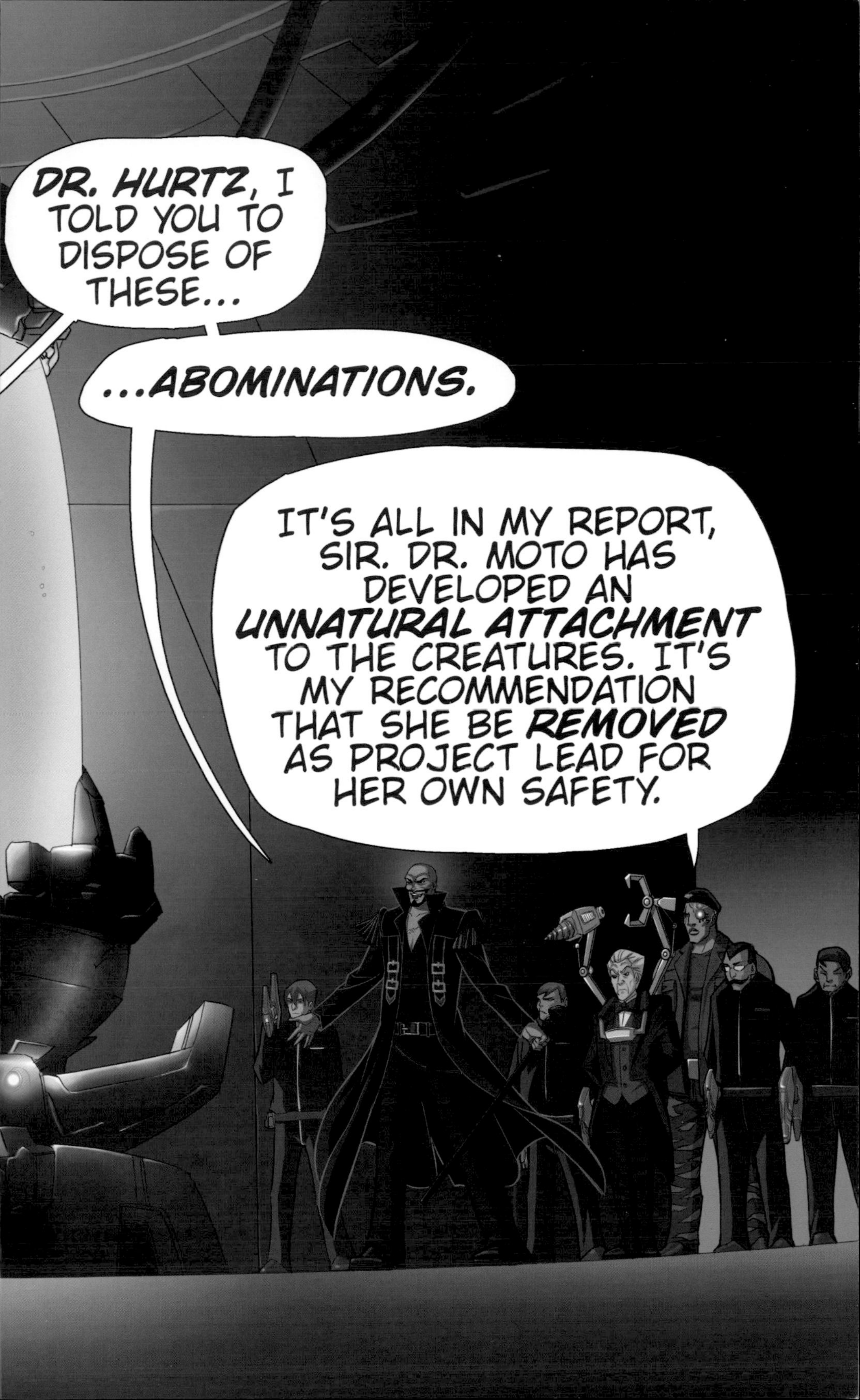
DR. HURTZ, I TOLD YOU TO DISPOSE OF THESE...
...ABOMINATIONS.
IT'S ALL IN MY REPORT, SIR. DR. MOTO HAS DEVELOPED AN UNNATURAL ATTACHMENT TO THE CREATURES. IT'S MY RECOMMENDATION THAT SHE BE REMOVED AS PROJECT LEAD FOR HER OWN SAFETY.

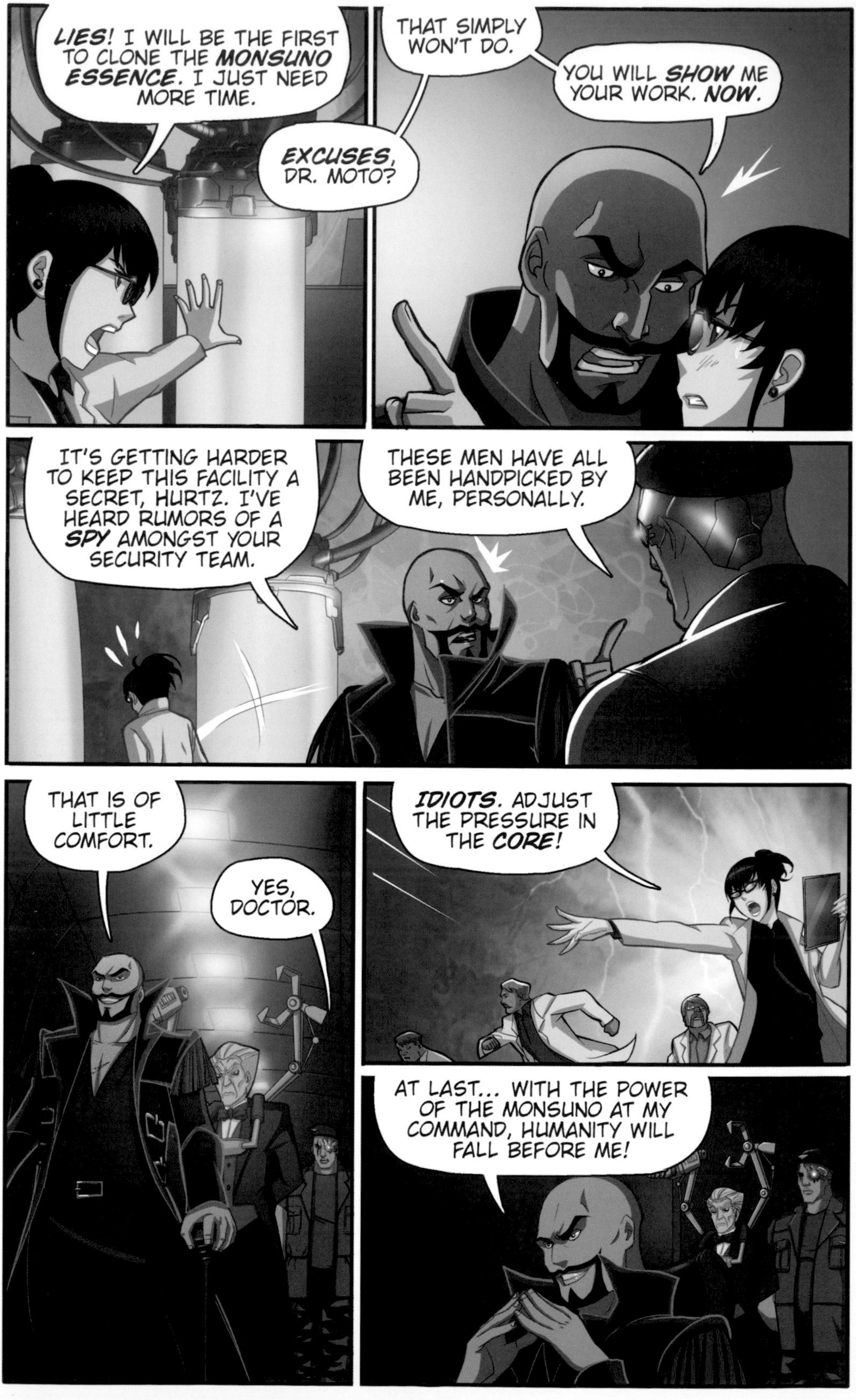
LIES! I WILL BE THE FIRST TO CLONE THE MONSUNO ESSENCE. I JUST NEED MORE TIME.
THAT SIMPLY WON'T DO.
EXCUSES, DR. MOTO?
YOU WILL SHOW ME YOUR WORK. NOW.
IT'S GETTING HARDER TO KEEP THIS FACILITY A SECRET, HURTZ. I'VE HEARD RUMORS OF A SPY AMONGST YOUR SECURITY TEAM.
THESE MEN HAVE ALL BEEN HANDPICKED BY ME, PERSONALLY.
THAT IS OF LITTLE COMFORT.
YES, DOCTOR.
IDIOTS. ADJUST THE PRESSURE IN THE CORE!
AT LAST... WITH THE POWER OF THE MONSUNO AT MY COMMAND, HUMANITY WILL FALL BEFORE ME!

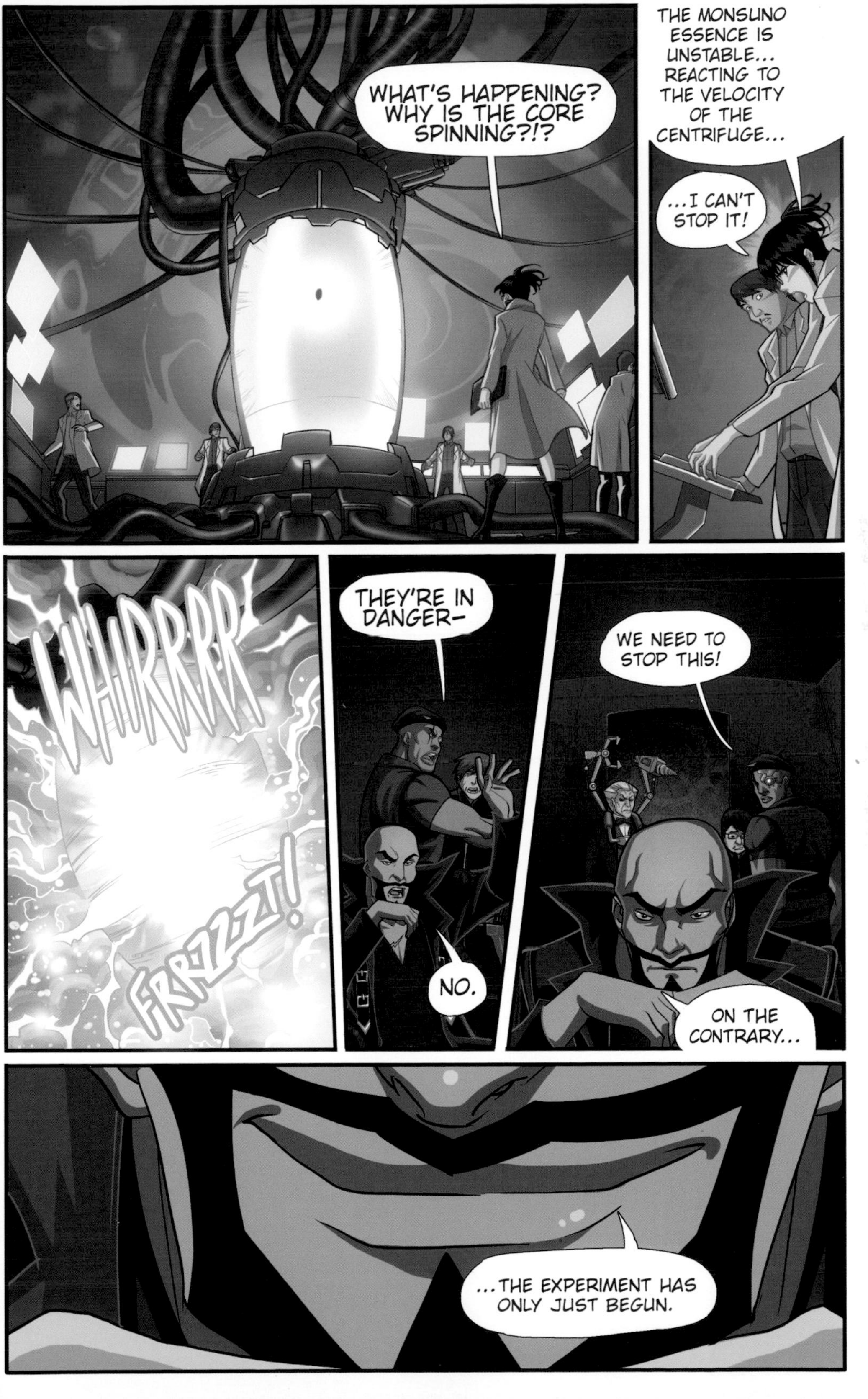
WHAT'S HAPPENING? WHY IS THE CORE SPINNING?!?
THE MONSUNO ESSENCE IS UNSTABLE... REACTING TO THE VELOCITY OF THE CENTRIFUGE...
...I CAN'T STOP IT!
WHIRRRR
FRRZZZT!
THEY'RE IN DANGER–
NO.
WE NEED TO STOP THIS!
ON THE CONTRARY...
...THE EXPERIMENT HAS ONLY JUST BEGUN.

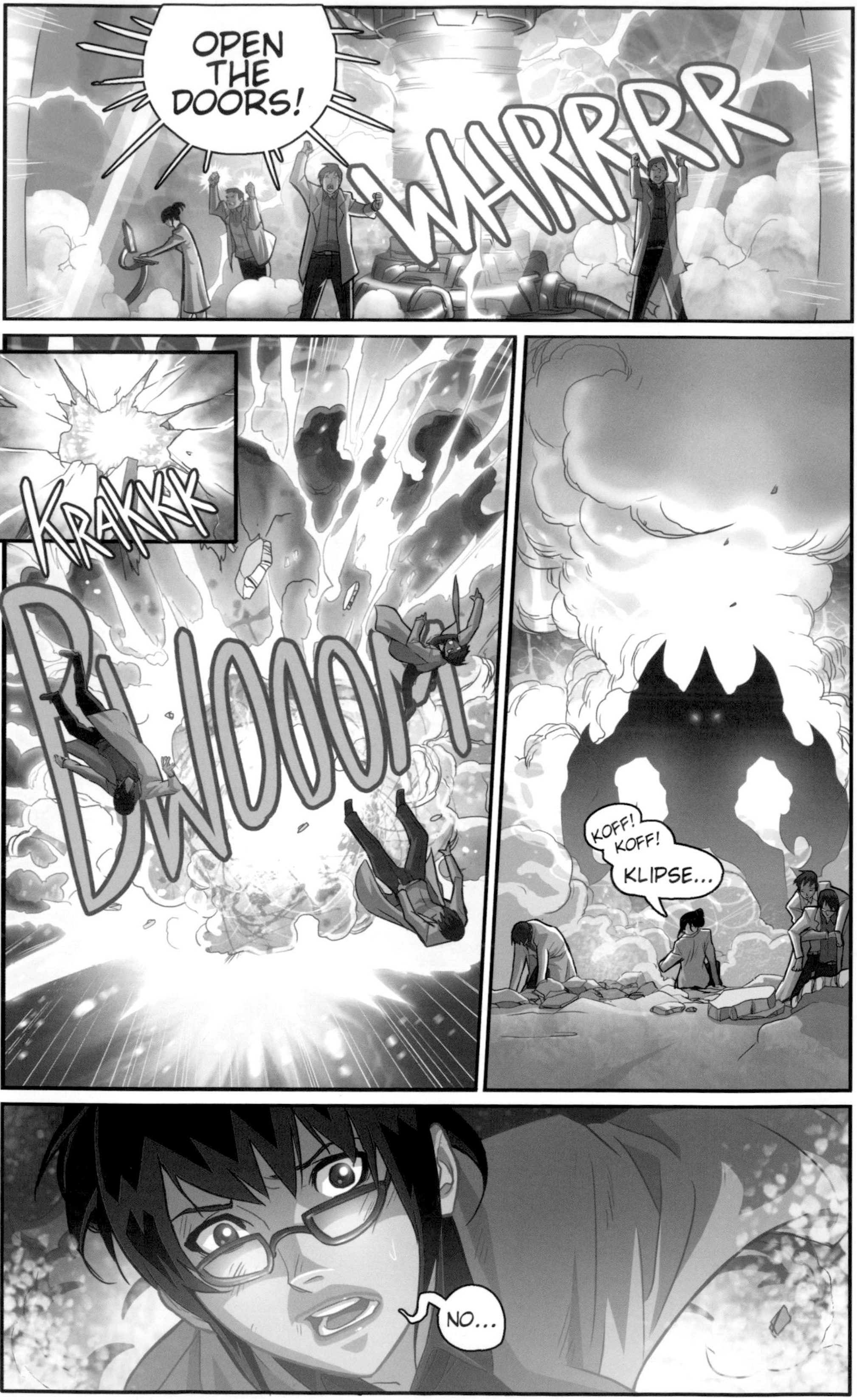
OPEN THE DOORS!
WHRRRR
KRAKKK
BWOOOM
KOFF! KOFF!
KLIPSE...
NO...

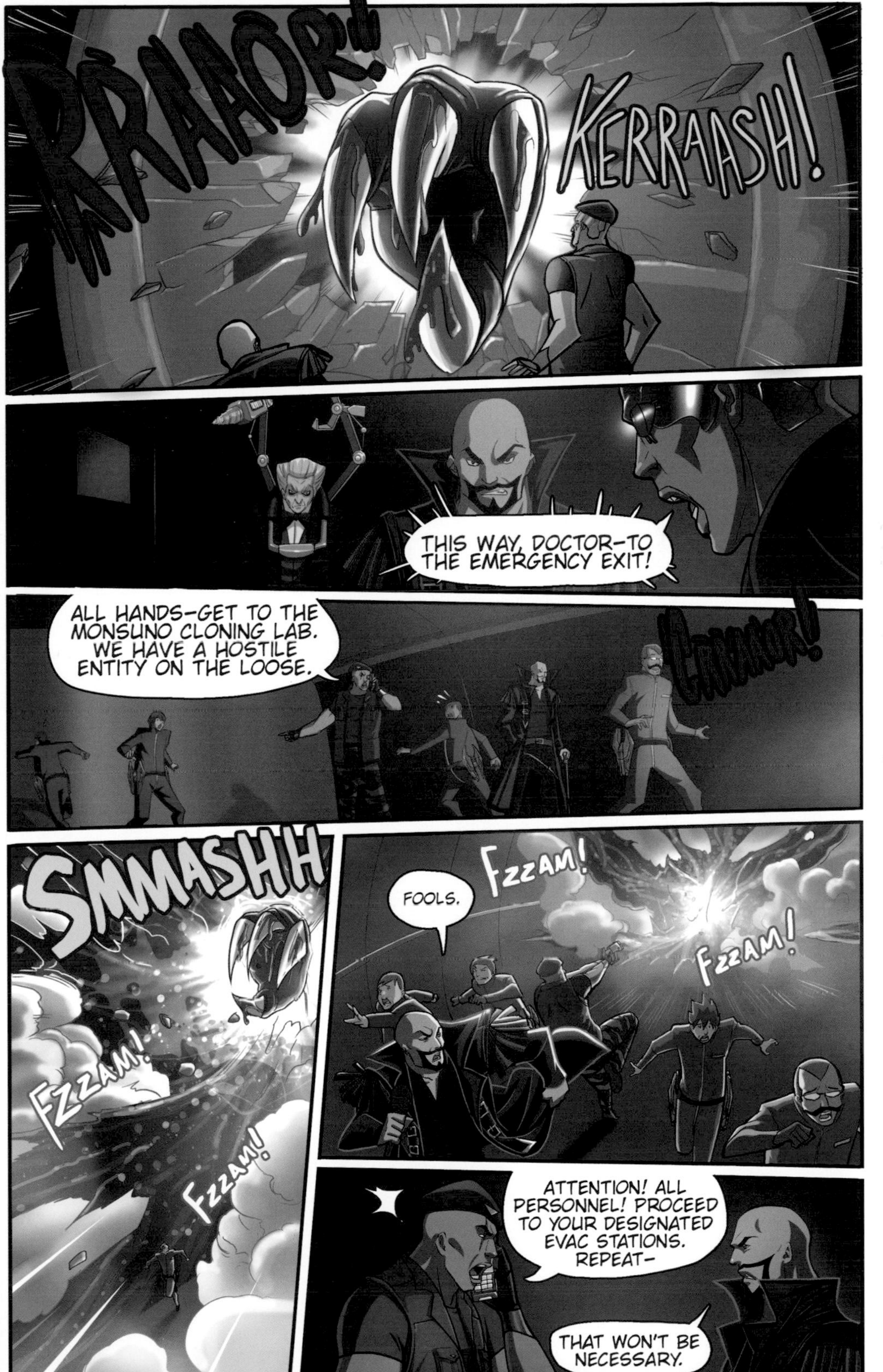
RRAAOR!!
KERRAASH!
THIS WAY, DOCTOR–TO THE EMERGENCY EXIT!
ALL HANDS–GET TO THE MONSUNO CLONING LAB. WE HAVE A HOSTILE ENTITY ON THE LOOSE.
SMMASHH
FZZAM!
FZZAM!
FOOLS.
FZZAM!
FZZAM!
ATTENTION! ALL PERSONNEL! PROCEED TO YOUR DESIGNATED EVAC STATIONS. REPEAT–
THAT WON'T BE NECESSARY.

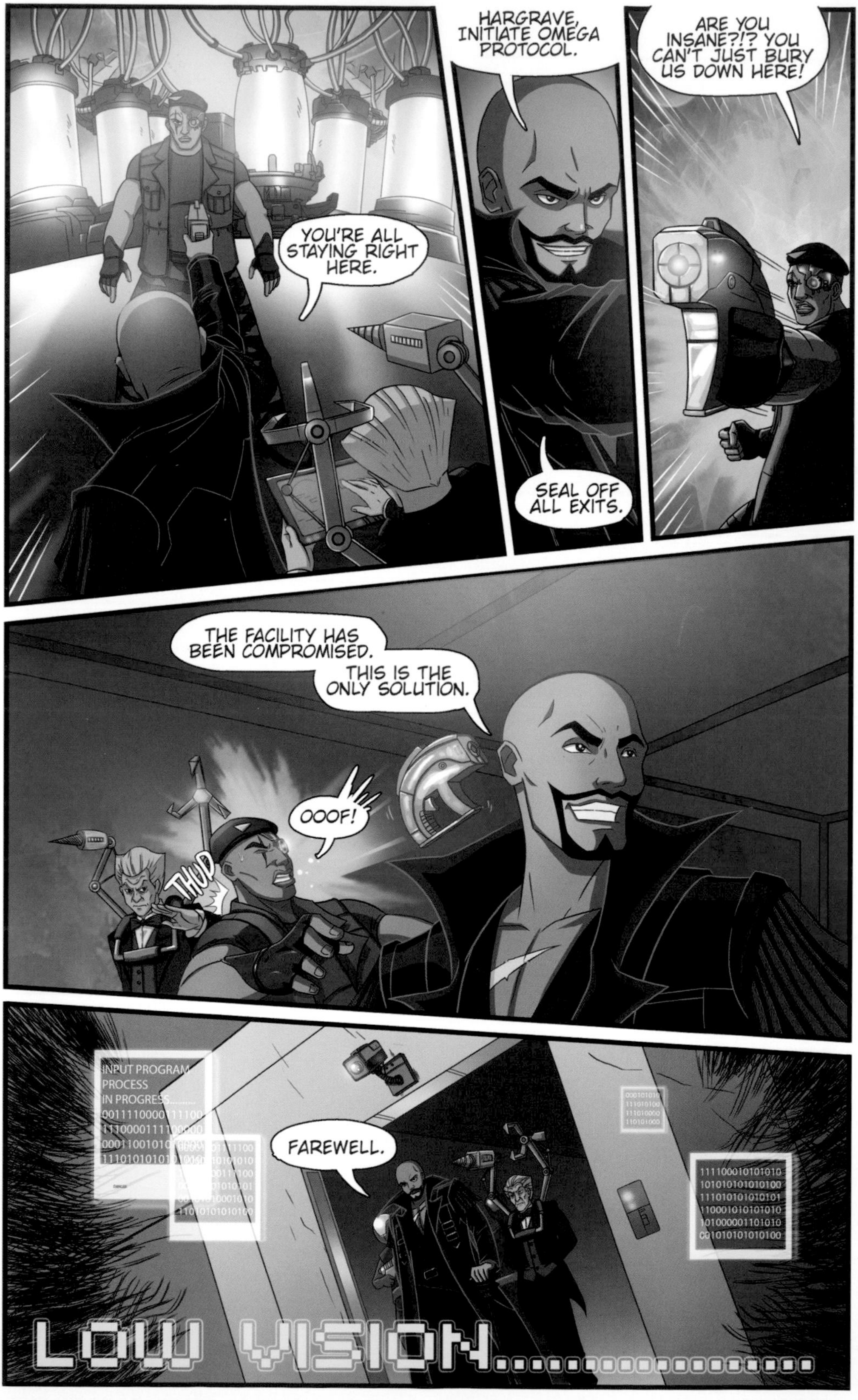
YOU'RE ALL STAYING RIGHT HERE.
HARGRAVE, INITIATE OMEGA PROTOCOL.
SEAL OFF ALL EXITS.
ARE YOU INSANE?!? YOU CAN'T JUST BURY US DOWN HERE!
THE FACILITY HAS BEEN COMPROMISED.
THIS IS THE ONLY SOLUTION.
OOOF!
THUD
INPUT PROGRAM
PROCESS
IN PROGRESS.........
FAREWELL.
LOW VISION.................

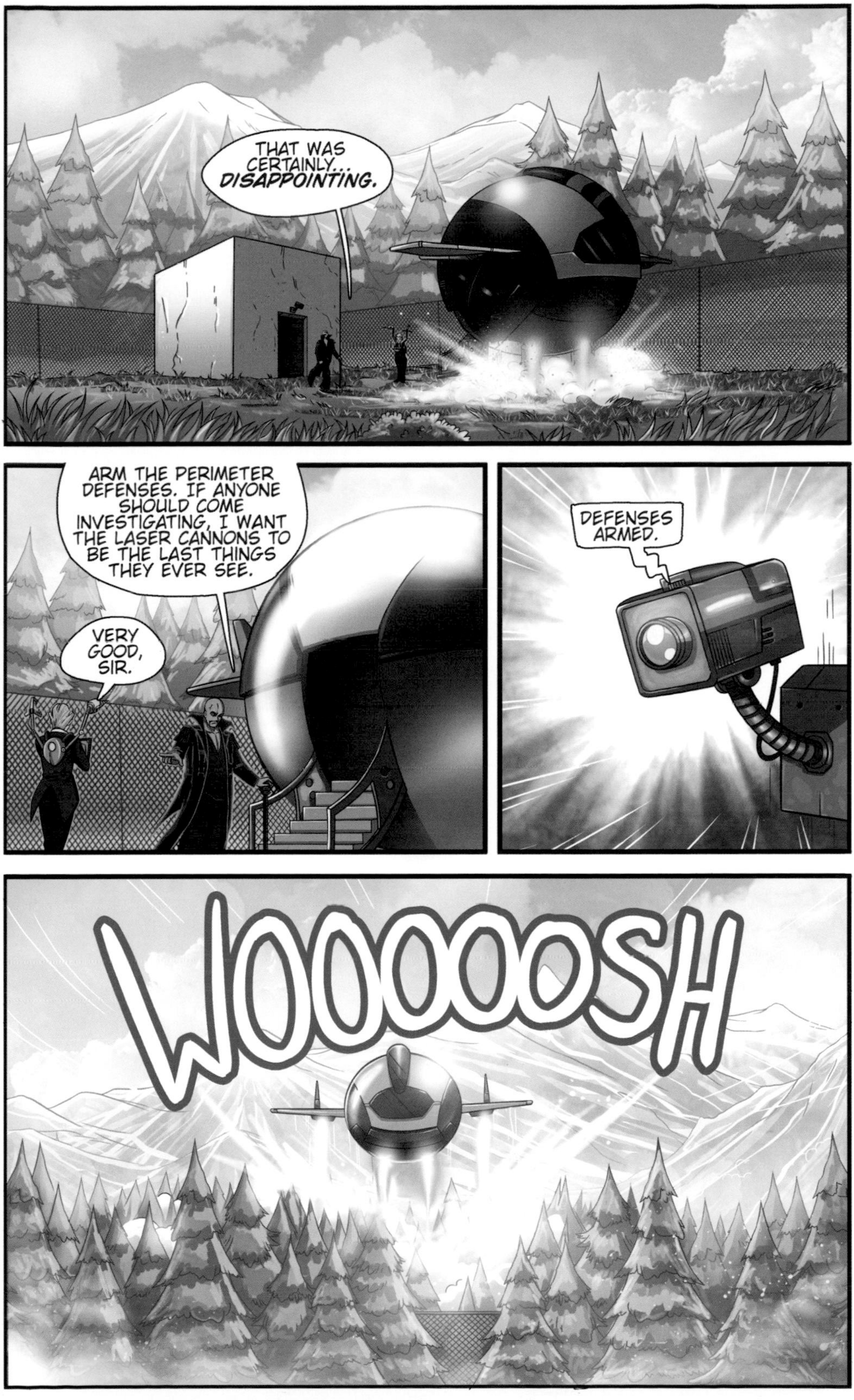
THAT WAS CERTAINLY... *DISAPPOINTING.*
ARM THE PERIMETER DEFENSES. IF ANYONE SHOULD COME INVESTIGATING, I WANT THE LASER CANNONS TO BE THE LAST THINGS THEY EVER SEE.
VERY GOOD, SIR.
DEFENSES ARMED.
WOOOOOSH

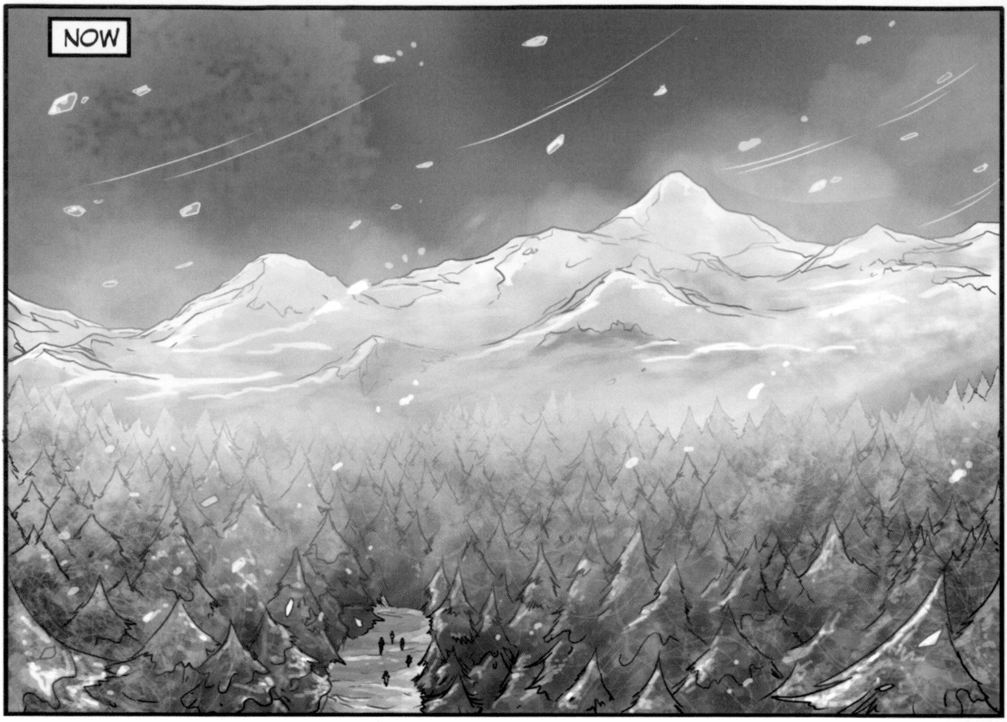
NOW

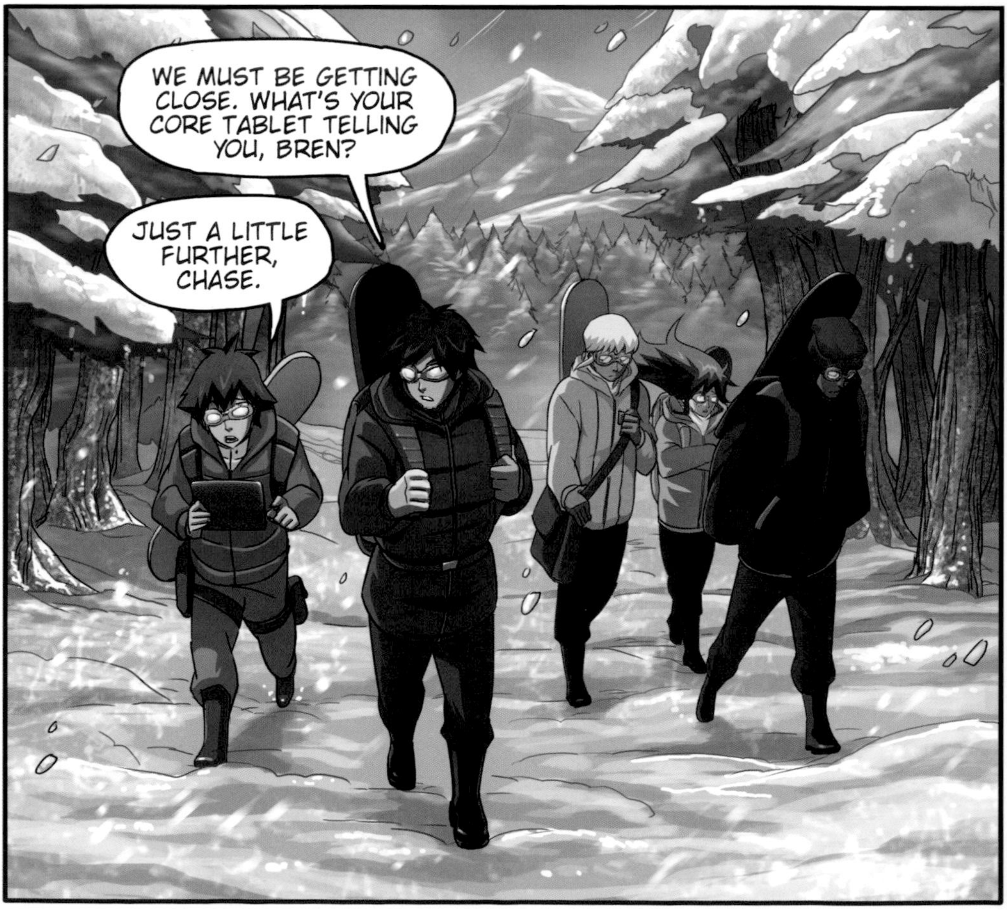
WE MUST BE GETTING CLOSE. WHAT'S YOUR CORE TABLET TELLING YOU, BREN?
JUST A LITTLE FURTHER, CHASE.

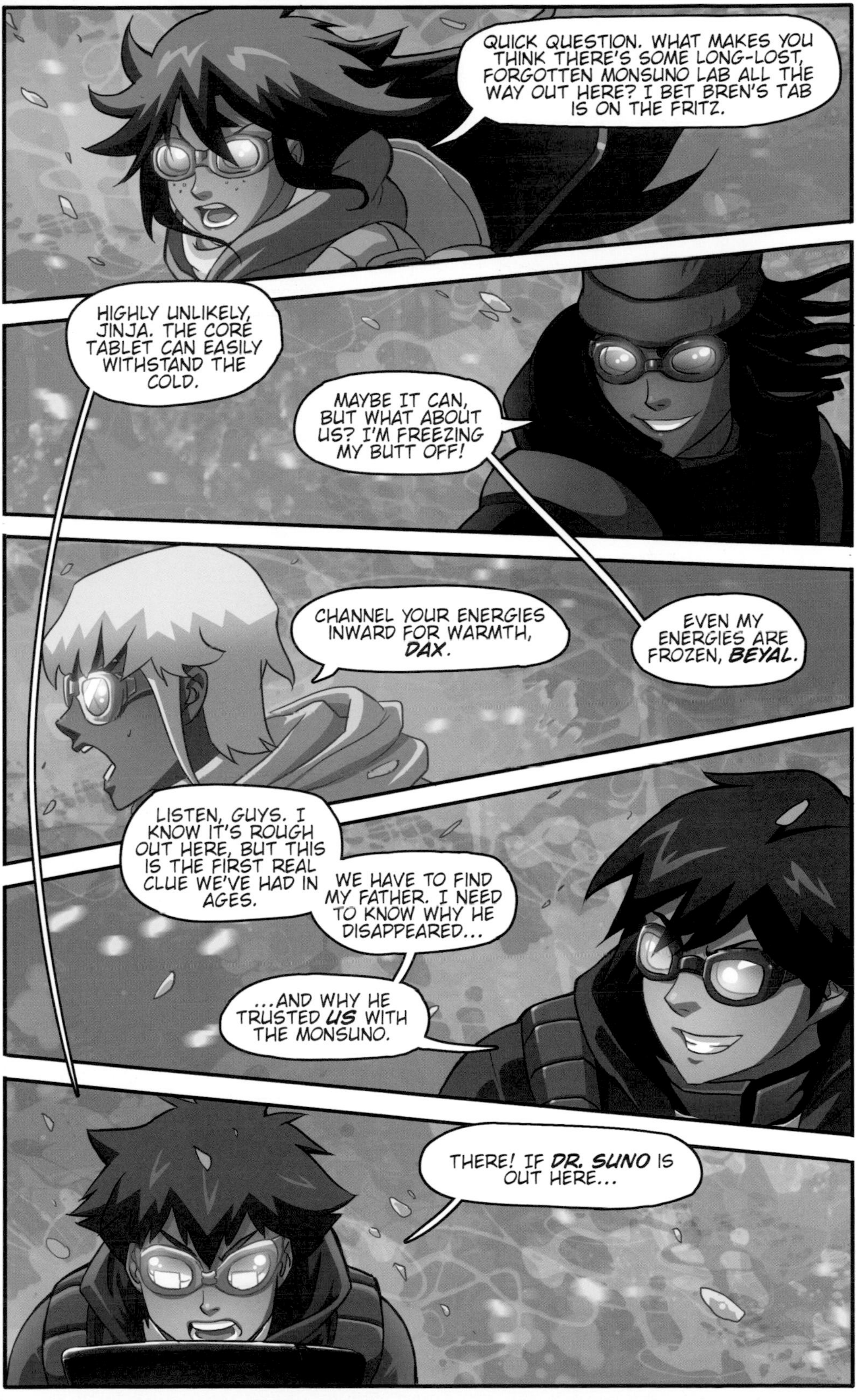
QUICK QUESTION. WHAT MAKES YOU THINK THERE'S SOME LONG-LOST, FORGOTTEN MONSUNO LAB ALL THE WAY OUT HERE? I BET BREN'S TAB IS ON THE FRITZ.
HIGHLY UNLIKELY, JINJA. THE CORE TABLET CAN EASILY WITHSTAND THE COLD.
MAYBE IT CAN, BUT WHAT ABOUT US? I'M FREEZING MY BUTT OFF!
CHANNEL YOUR ENERGIES INWARD FOR WARMTH, DAX.
EVEN MY ENERGIES ARE FROZEN, BEYAL.
LISTEN, GUYS. I KNOW IT'S ROUGH OUT HERE, BUT THIS IS THE FIRST REAL CLUE WE'VE HAD IN AGES.
WE HAVE TO FIND MY FATHER. I NEED TO KNOW WHY HE DISAPPEARED...
...AND WHY HE TRUSTED US WITH THE MONSUNO.
THERE! IF DR. SUNO IS OUT HERE...

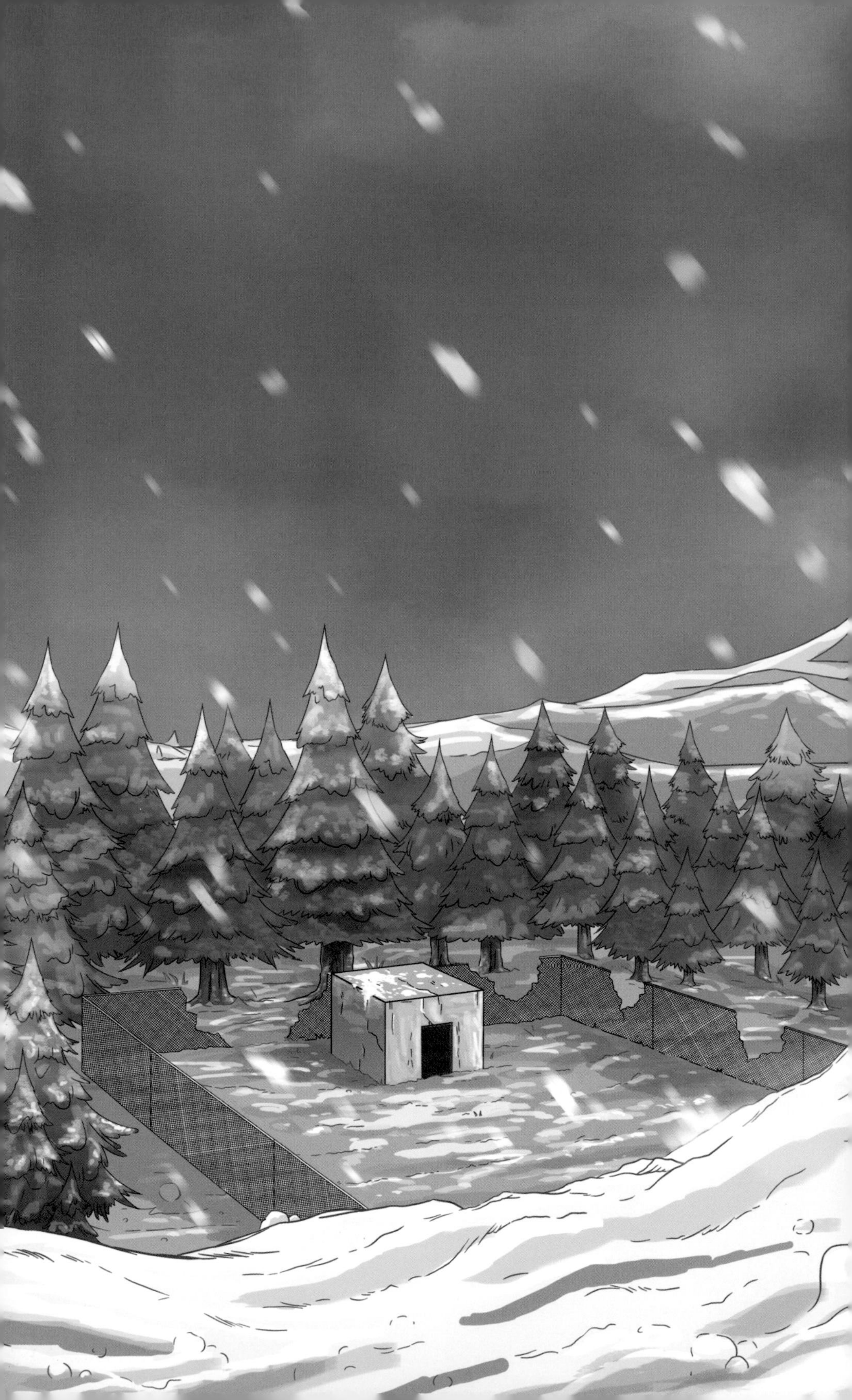

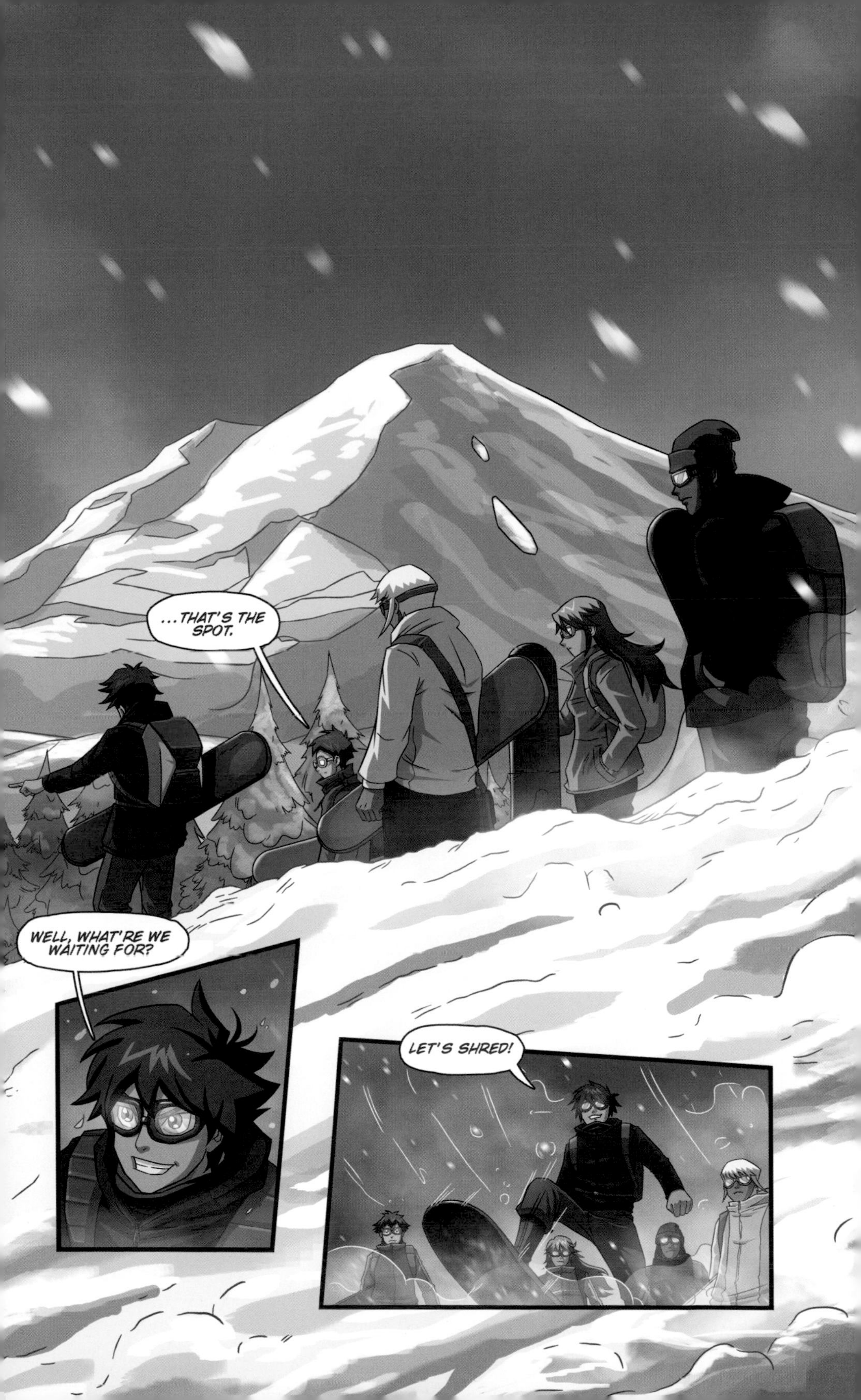
...THAT'S THE SPOT.
WELL, WHAT'RE WE WAITING FOR?
LET'S SHRED!

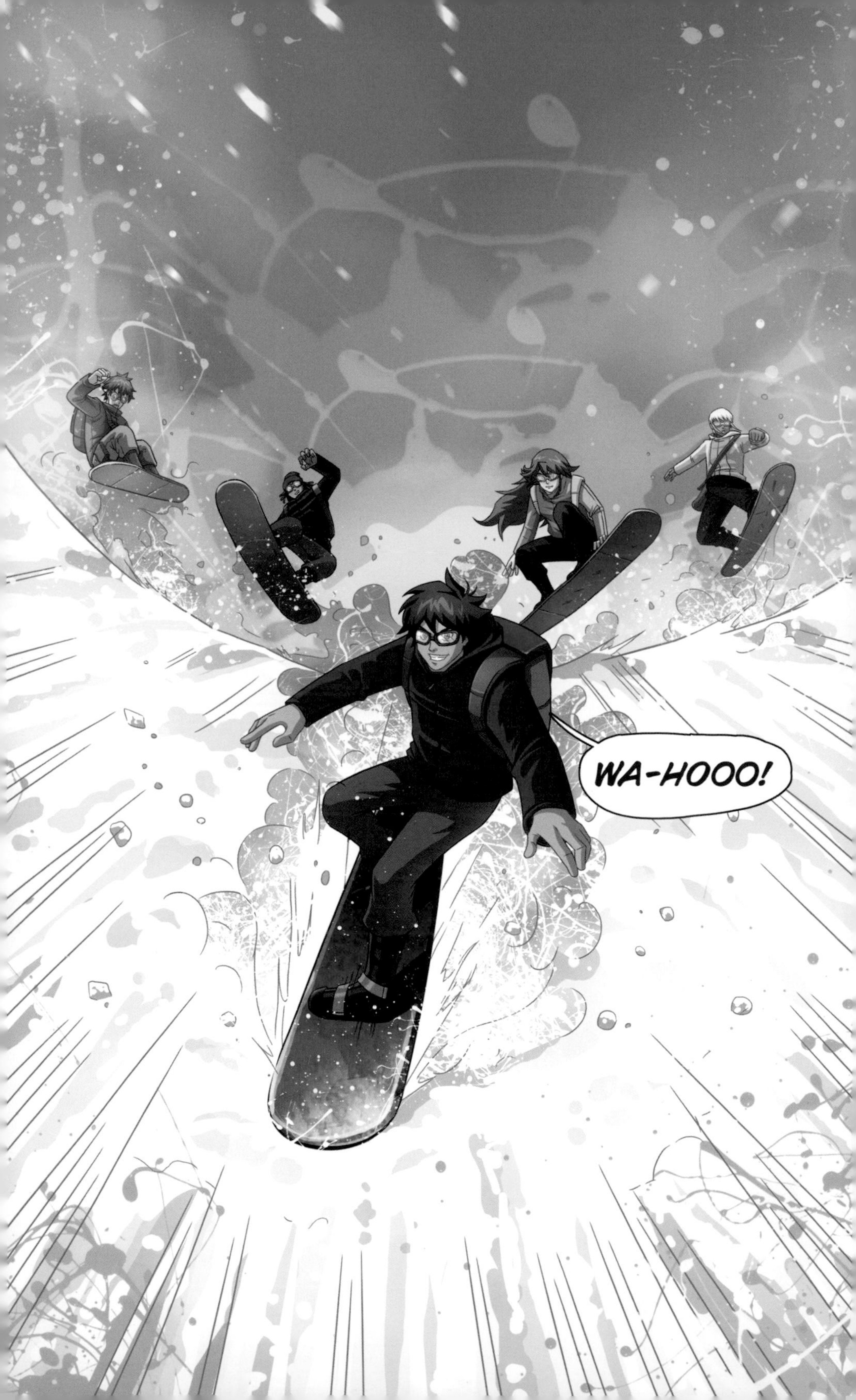
WA-HOOO!

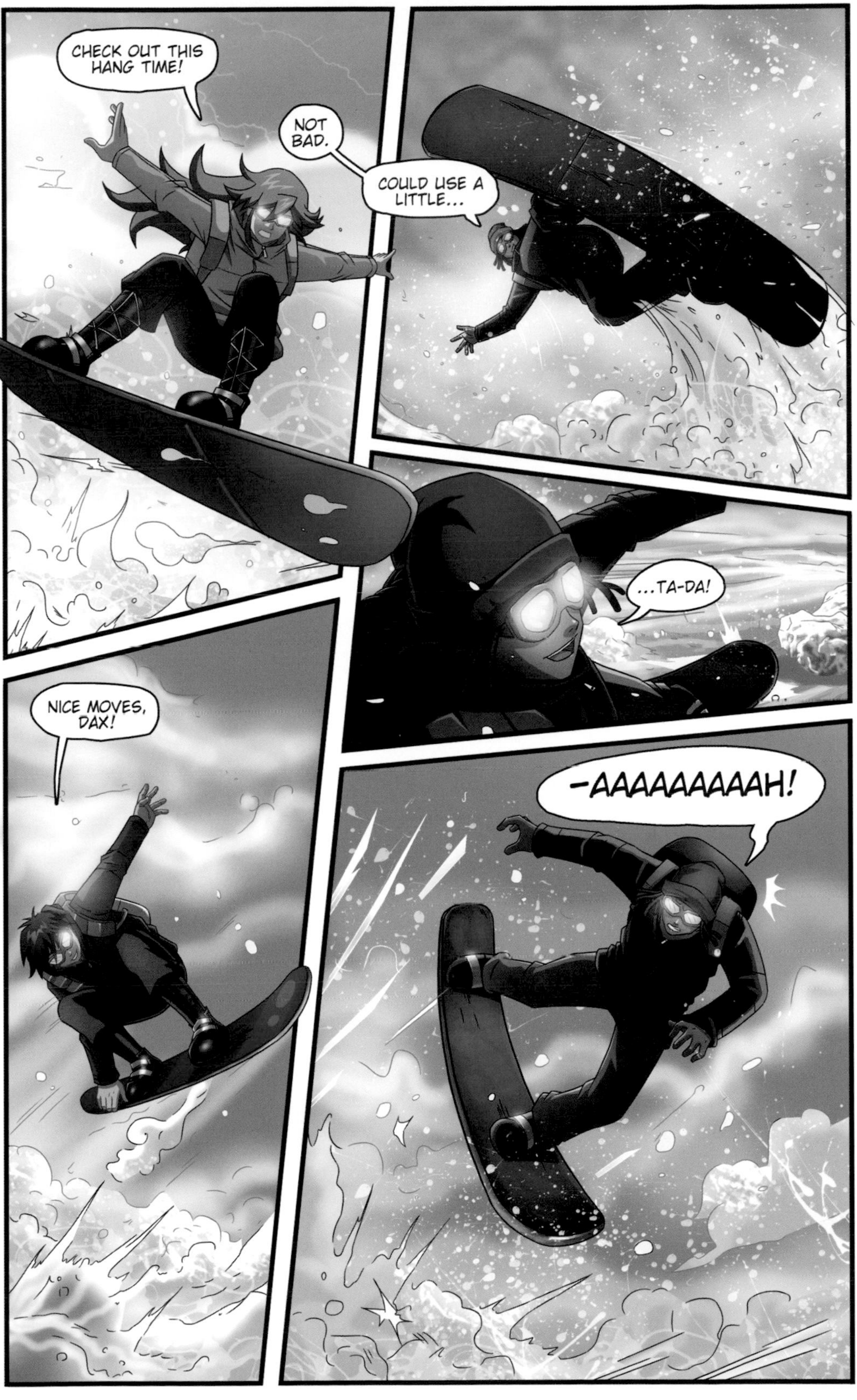
CHECK OUT THIS HANG TIME!
NOT BAD.
COULD USE A LITTLE...
...TA-DA!
NICE MOVES, DAX!
-AAAAAAAAAH!

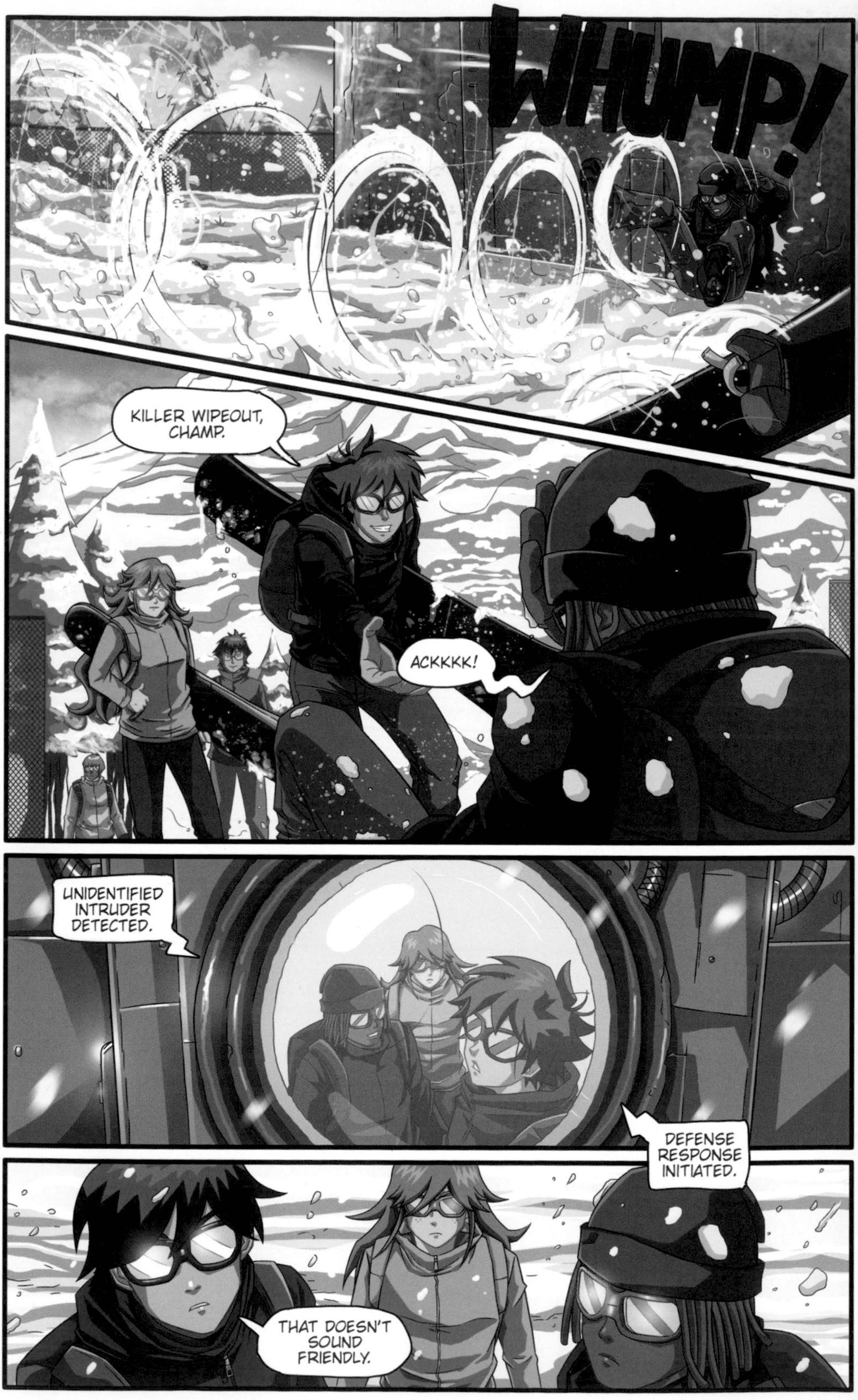
WHUMP!
KILLER WIPEOUT, CHAMP.
ACKKKK!
UNIDENTIFIED INTRUDER DETECTED.
DEFENSE RESPONSE INITIATED.
THAT DOESN'T SOUND FRIENDLY.

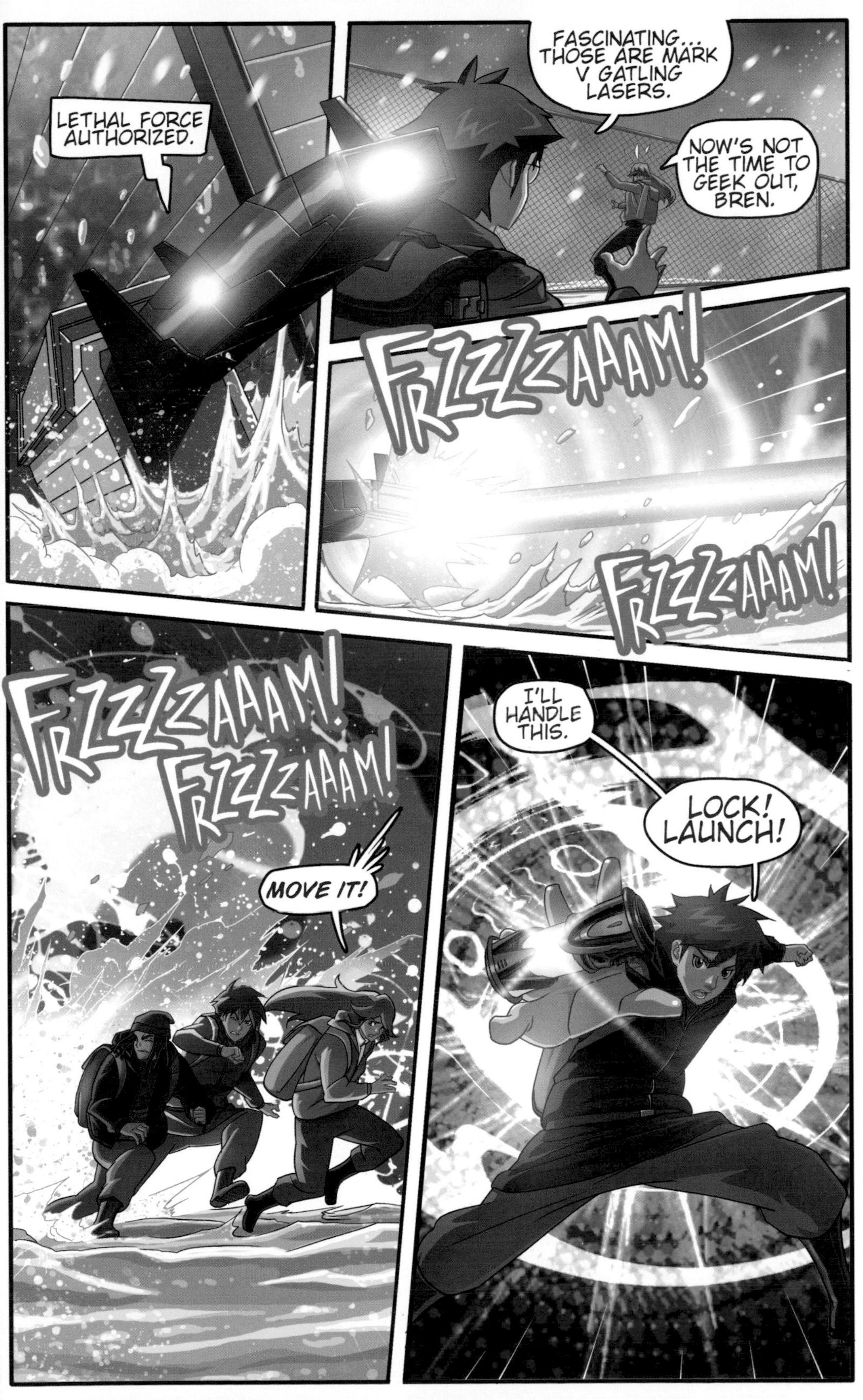
LETHAL FORCE AUTHORIZED.
FASCINATING... THOSE ARE MARK V GATLING LASERS.
NOW'S NOT THE TIME TO GEEK OUT, BREN.
FRZZZAAAM!
FRZZZAAAM!
FRZZZAAAM!
FRZZZAAAM!
MOVE IT!
I'LL HANDLE THIS.
LOCK! LAUNCH!

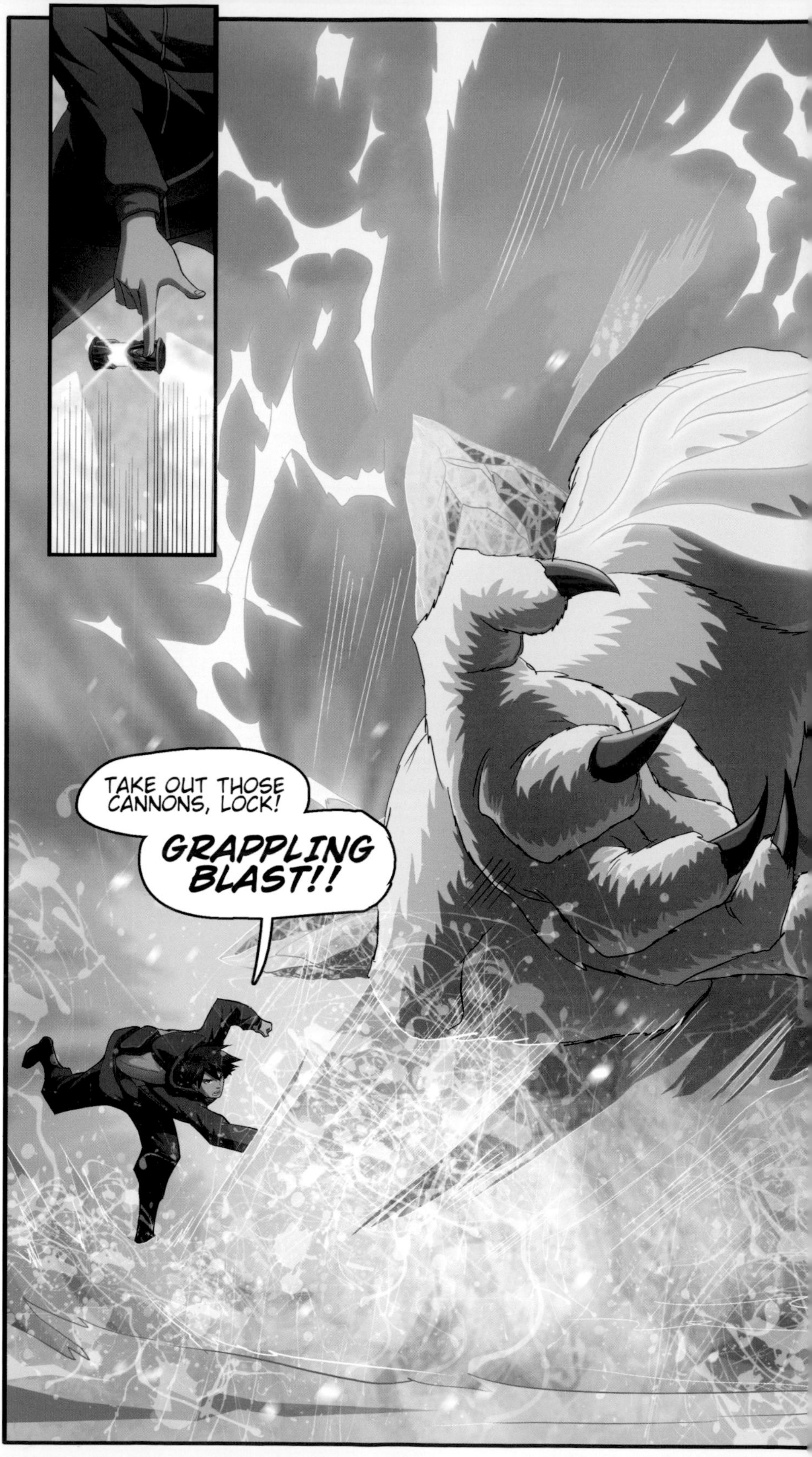
TAKE OUT THOSE CANNONS, LOCK!
GRAPPLING BLAST!!

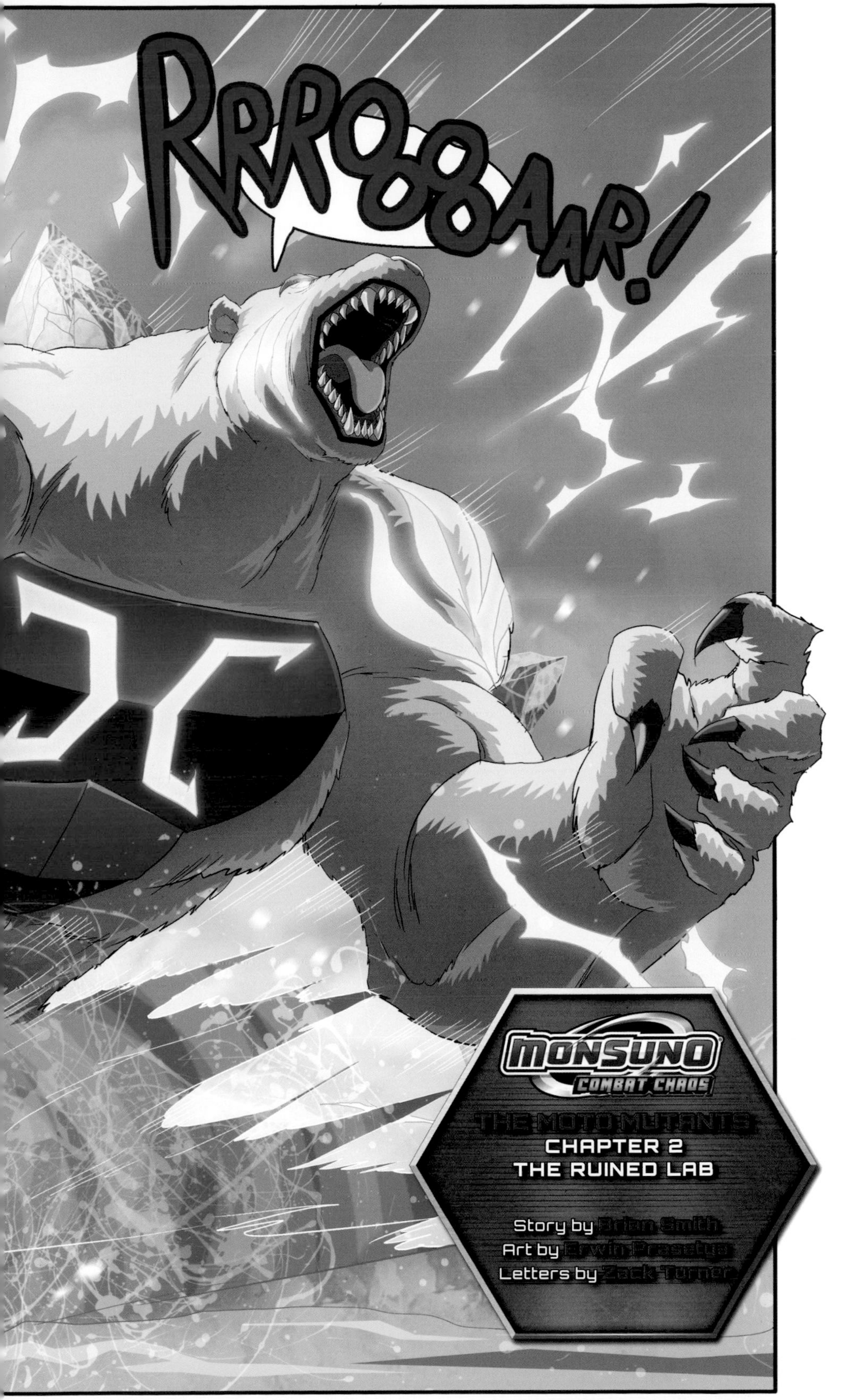
RRROOOOAAR!
MONSUNO
COMBAT CHAOS
THE MOTO MUTANTS
CHAPTER 2
THE RUINED LAB
Story by Brian Smith
Art by Erwin Prasetya
Letters by Zack Turner

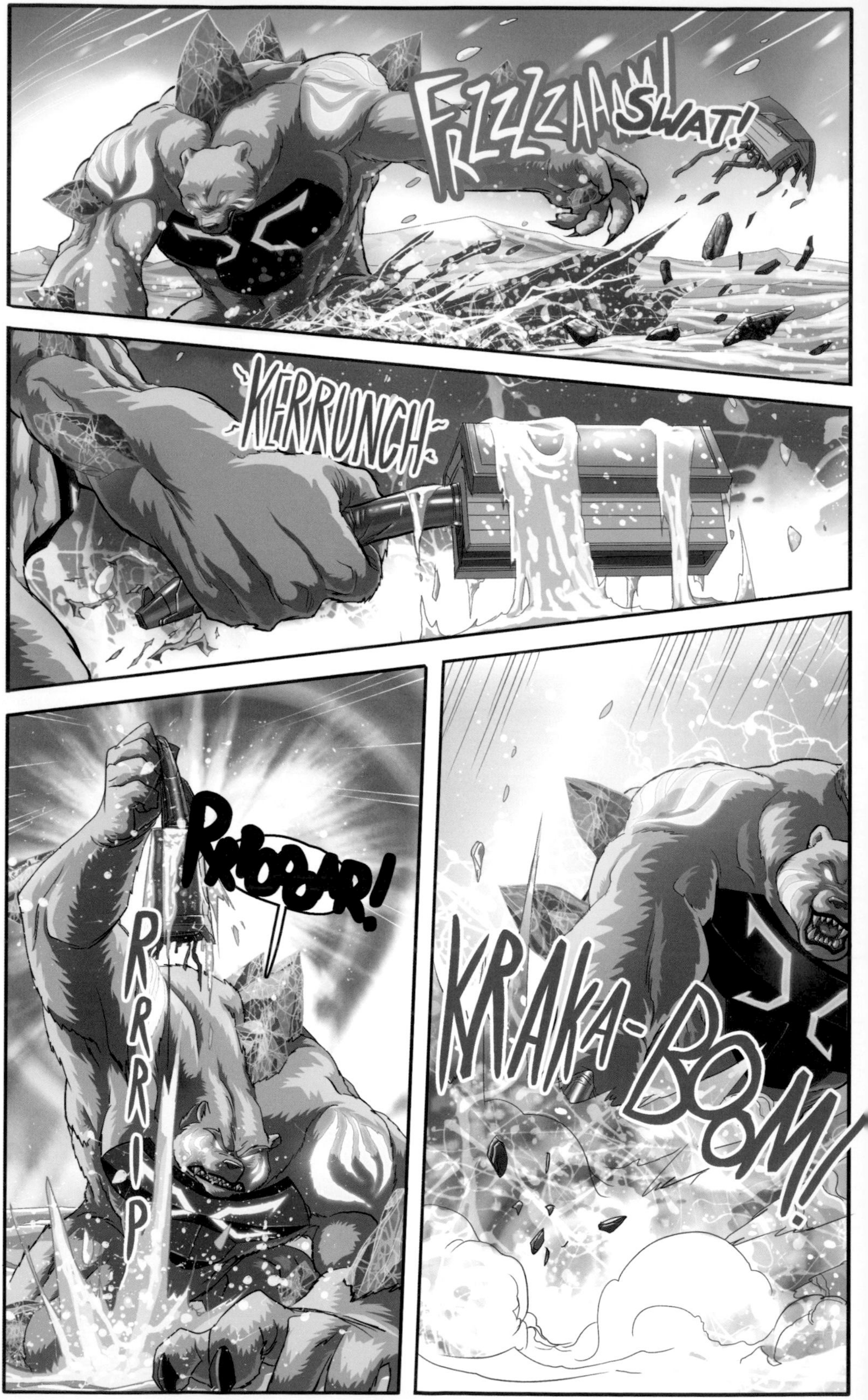
FRZZZAAM!
SWAT!
KERRUNCH
RROOAR!
RRRRIP
KRAKA-BOOM!

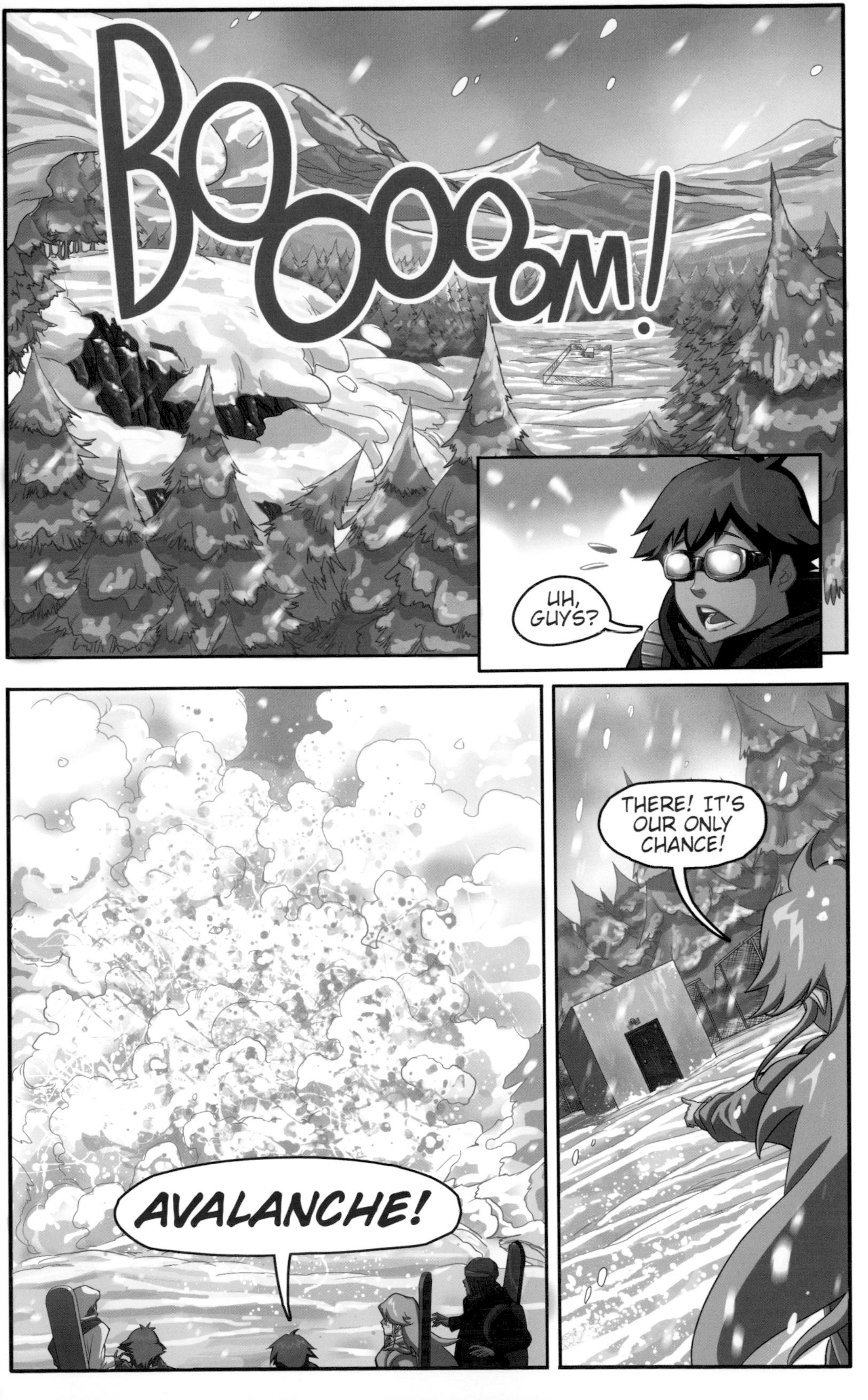
BOOOOOOM!
UH, GUYS?
AVALANCHE!
THERE! IT'S OUR ONLY CHANCE!

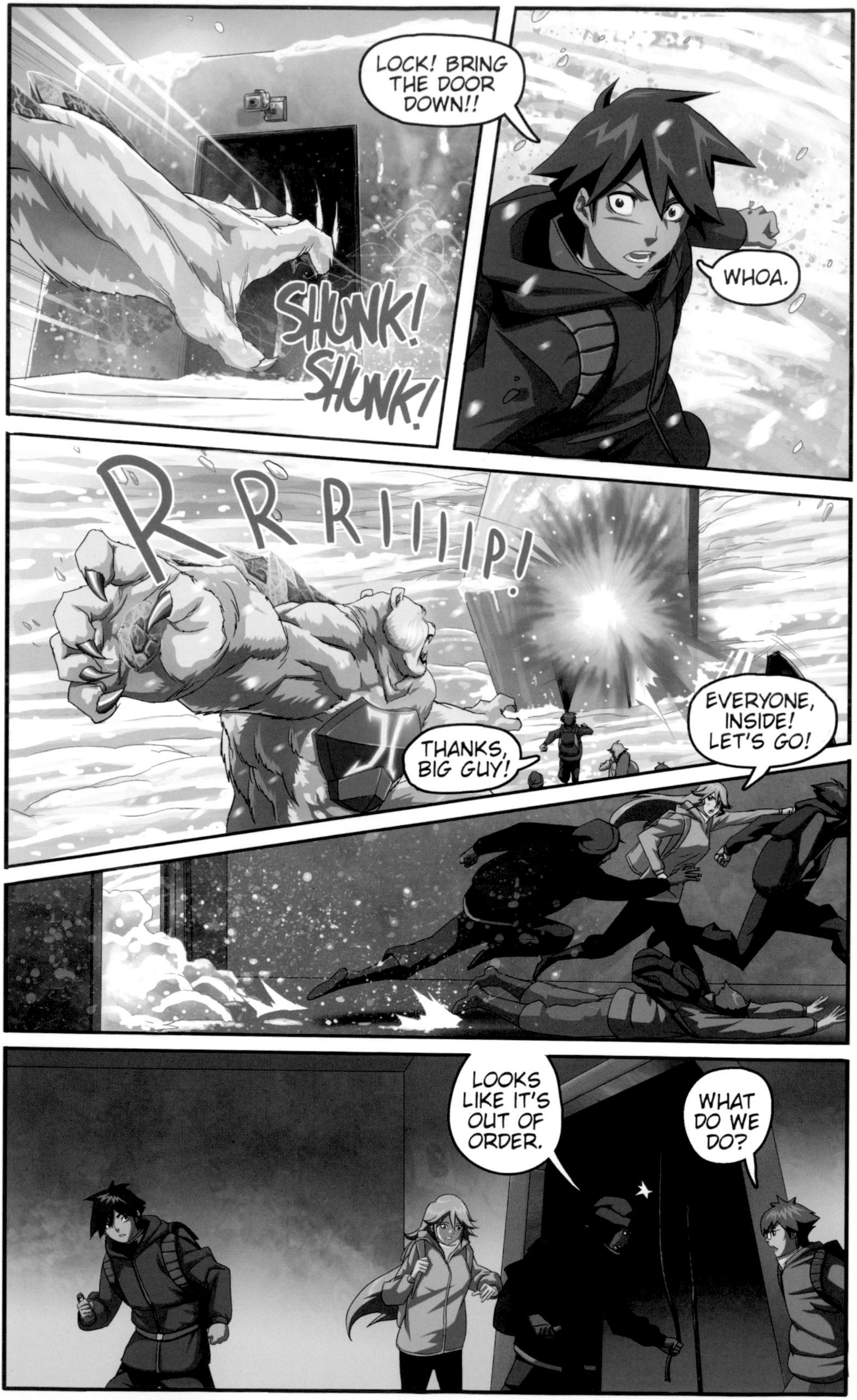
LOCK! BRING THE DOOR DOWN!!
SHUNK! SHUNK!
WHOA.
RRRIIIIP!
THANKS, BIG GUY!
EVERYONE, INSIDE! LET'S GO!
LOOKS LIKE IT'S OUT OF ORDER.
WHAT DO WE DO?

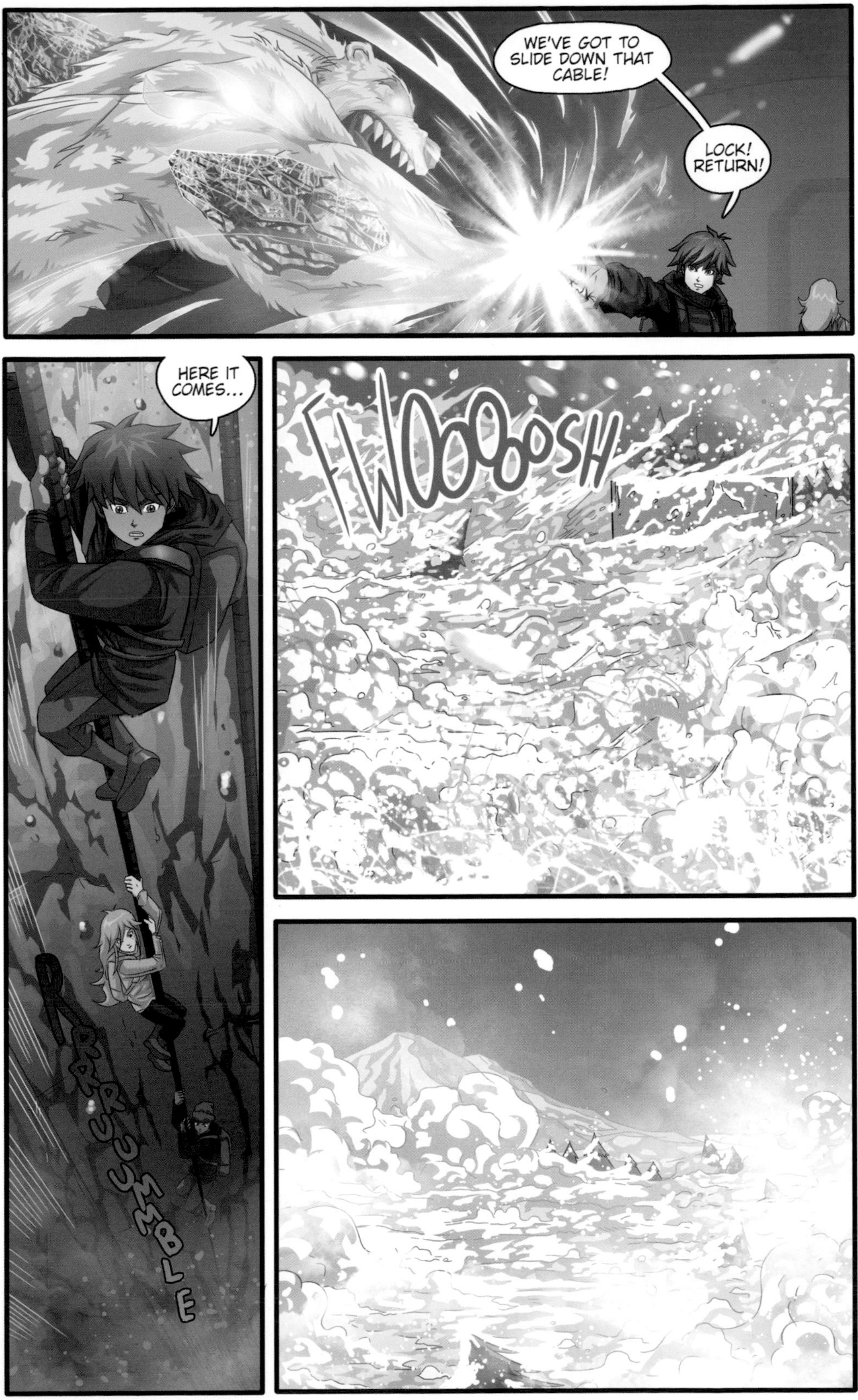
WE'VE GOT TO SLIDE DOWN THAT CABLE!
LOCK! RETURN!
HERE IT COMES...
FWOOOoOSH
RRRUUMMBLE

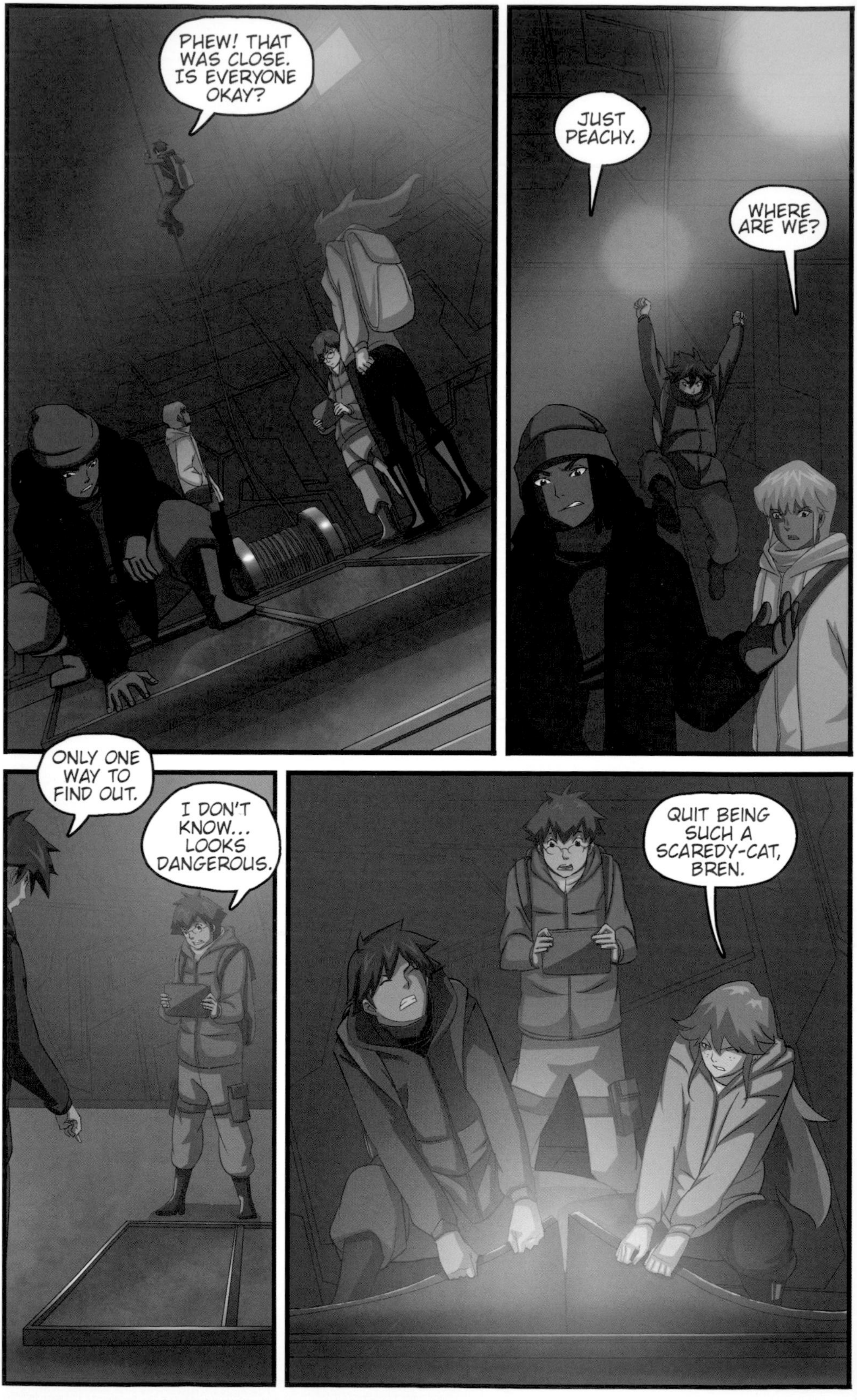
PHEW! THAT WAS CLOSE. IS EVERYONE OKAY?
JUST PEACHY.
WHERE ARE WE?
ONLY ONE WAY TO FIND OUT.
I DON'T KNOW... LOOKS DANGEROUS.
QUIT BEING SUCH A SCAREDY-CAT, BREN.

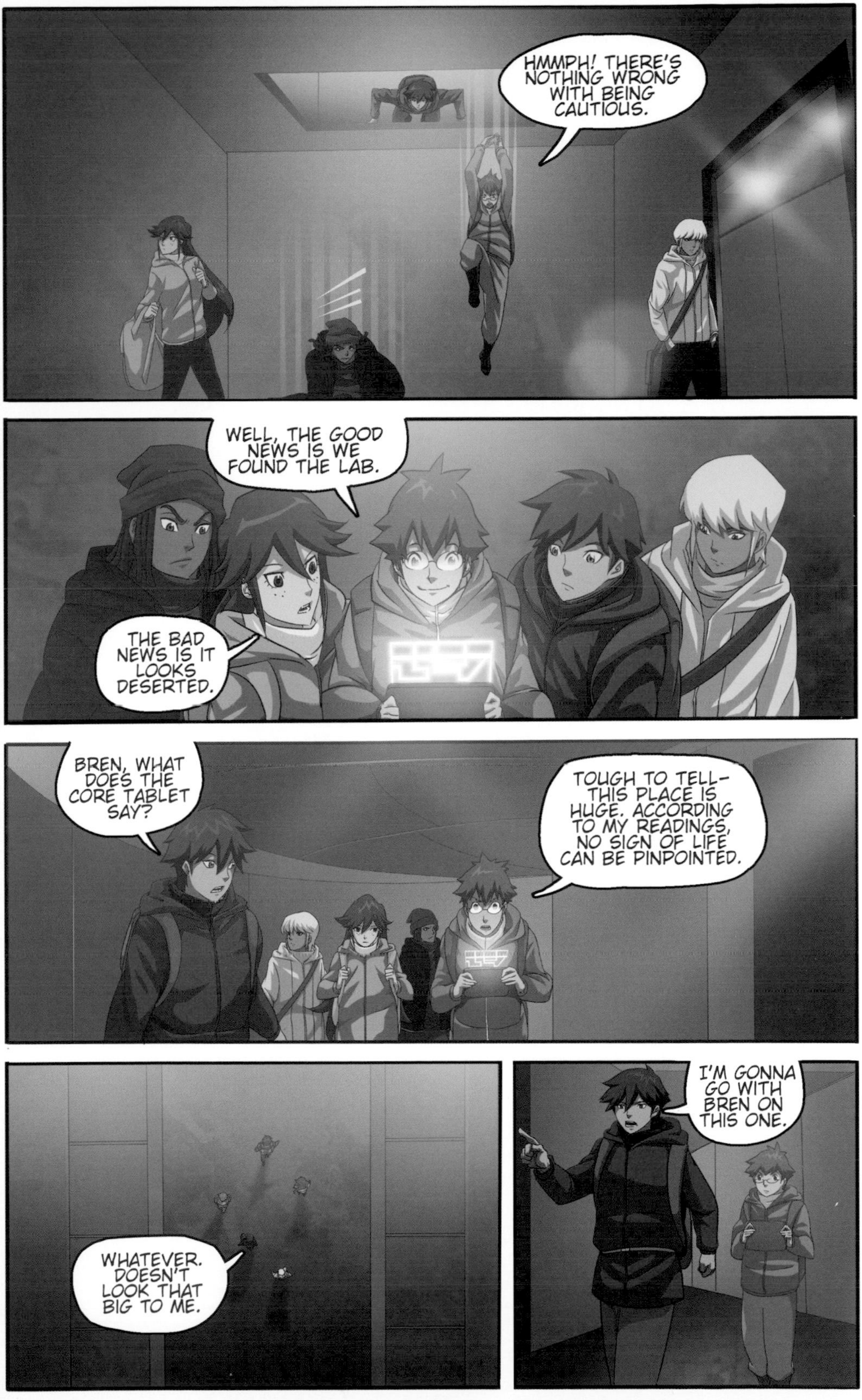
HMMPH! THERE'S NOTHING WRONG WITH BEING CAUTIOUS.
WELL, THE GOOD NEWS IS WE FOUND THE LAB.
THE BAD NEWS IS IT LOOKS DESERTED.
BREN, WHAT DOES THE CORE TABLET SAY?
TOUGH TO TELL- THIS PLACE IS HUGE. ACCORDING TO MY READINGS, NO SIGN OF LIFE CAN BE PINPOINTED.
WHATEVER. DOESN'T LOOK THAT BIG TO ME.
I'M GONNA GO WITH BREN ON THIS ONE.

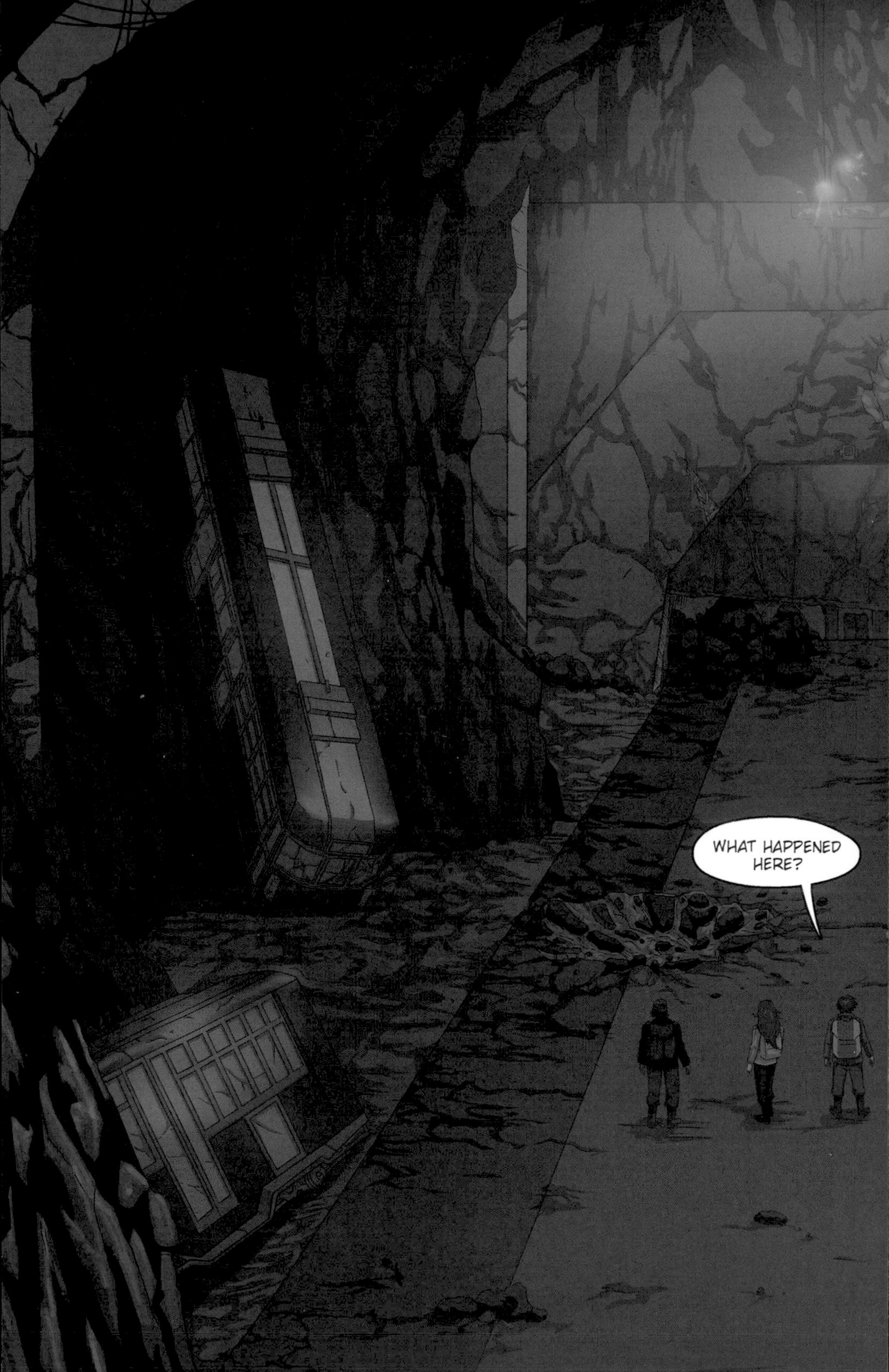
WHAT HAPPENED HERE?

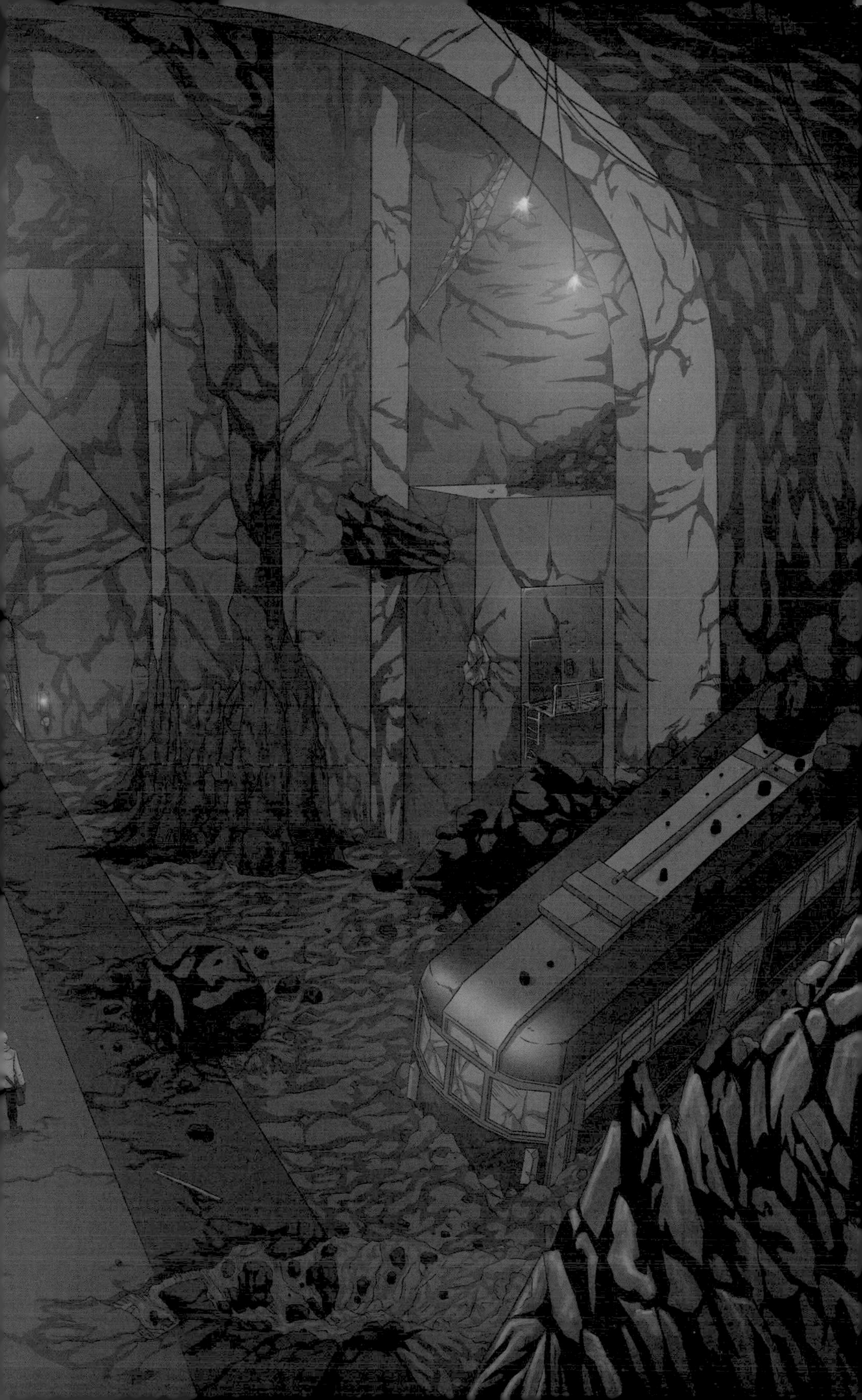

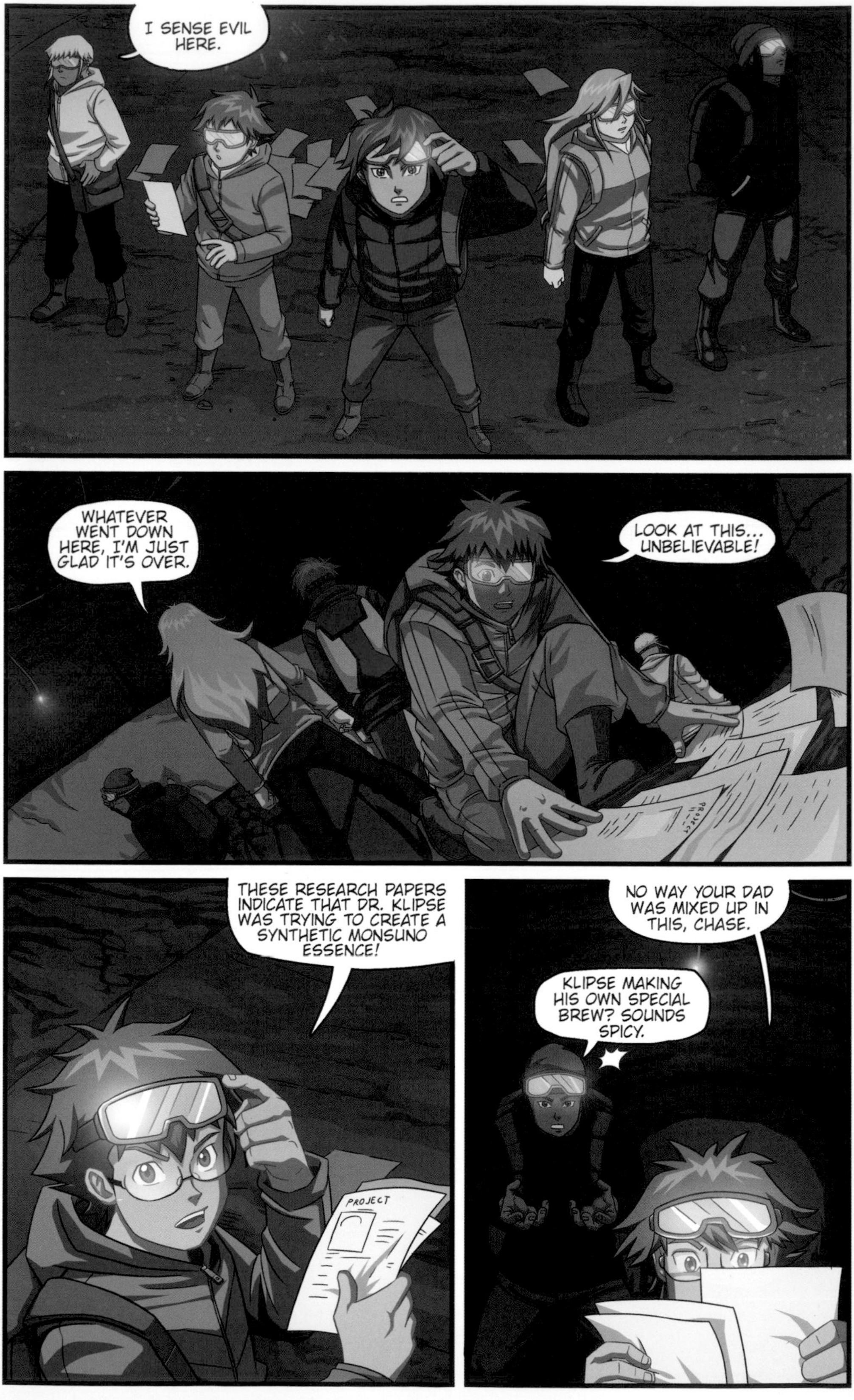
I SENSE EVIL HERE.
WHATEVER WENT DOWN HERE, I'M JUST GLAD IT'S OVER.
LOOK AT THIS... UNBELIEVABLE!
PROJECT
THESE RESEARCH PAPERS INDICATE THAT DR. KLIPSE WAS TRYING TO CREATE A SYNTHETIC MONSUNO ESSENCE!
PROJECT
NO WAY YOUR DAD WAS MIXED UP IN THIS, CHASE.
KLIPSE MAKING HIS OWN SPECIAL BREW? SOUNDS SPICY.

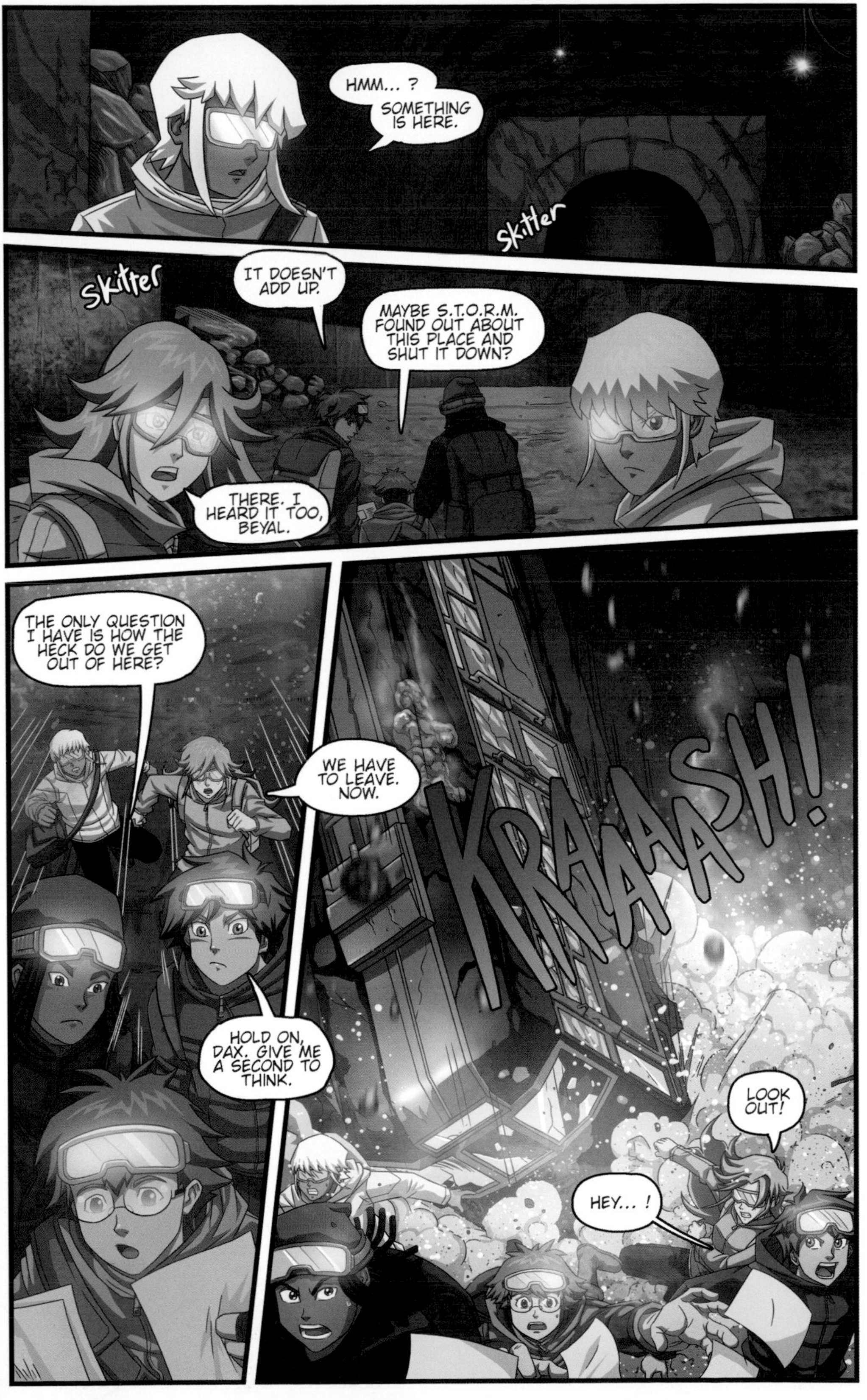
HMM... ?
SOMETHING IS HERE.
Skitter
Skitter
IT DOESN'T ADD UP.
MAYBE S.T.O.R.M. FOUND OUT ABOUT THIS PLACE AND SHUT IT DOWN?
THERE. I HEARD IT TOO, BEYAL.
THE ONLY QUESTION I HAVE IS HOW THE HECK DO WE GET OUT OF HERE?
WE HAVE TO LEAVE. NOW.
HOLD ON, DAX. GIVE ME A SECOND TO THINK.
KRAAASH!
LOOK OUT!
HEY... !

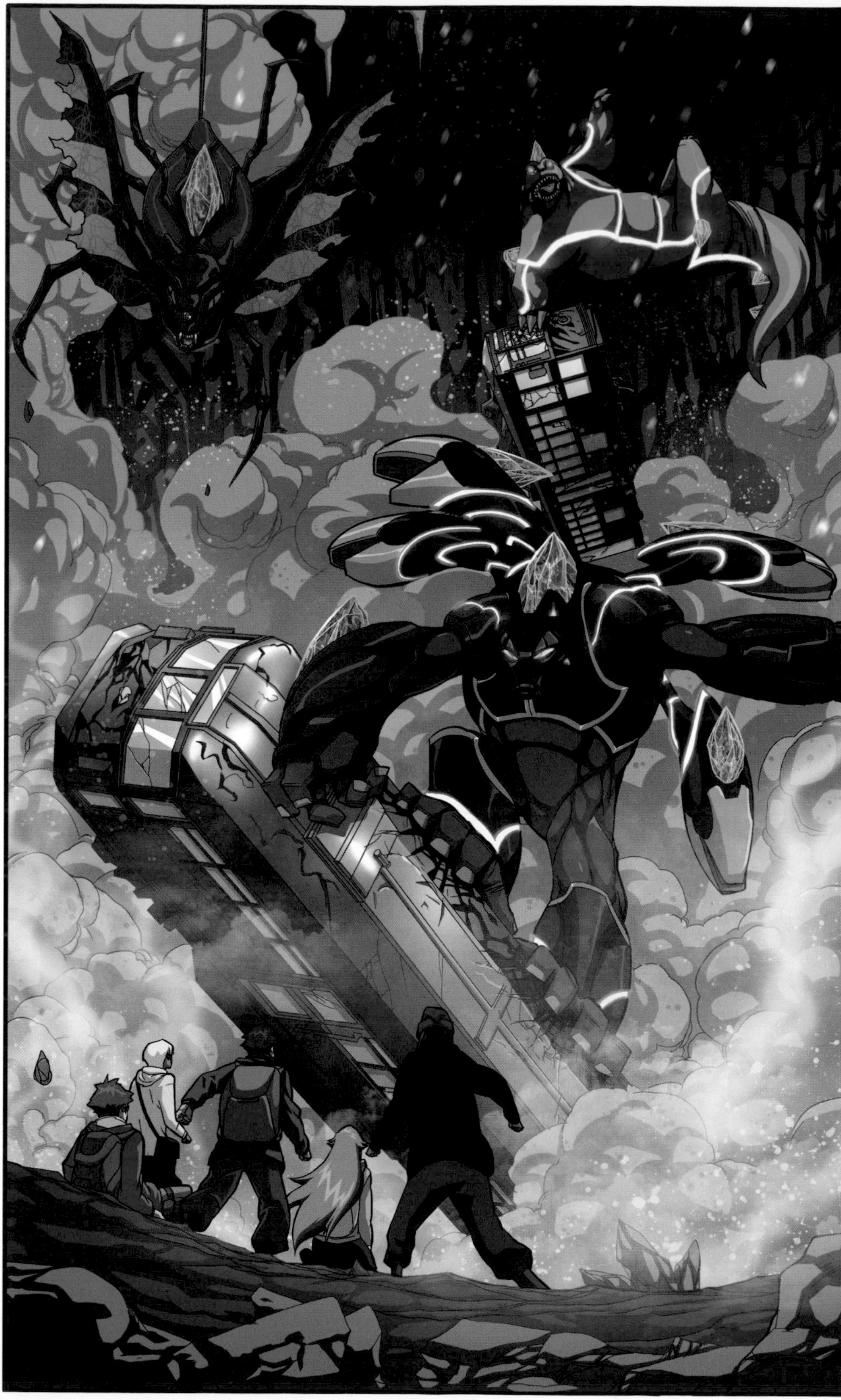

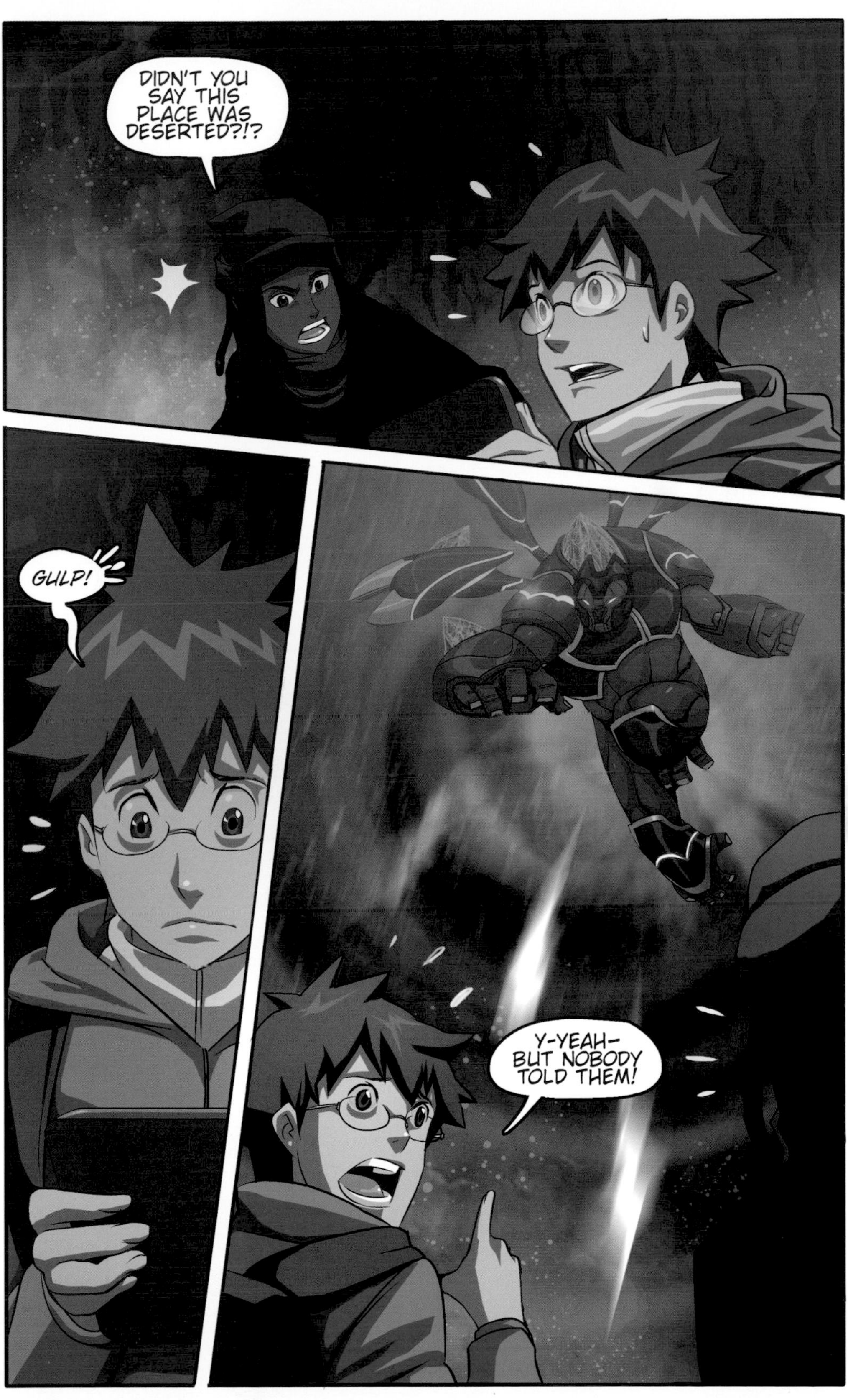
DIDN'T YOU SAY THIS PLACE WAS DESERTED?!?
GULP!
Y-YEAH--BUT NOBODY TOLD THEM!

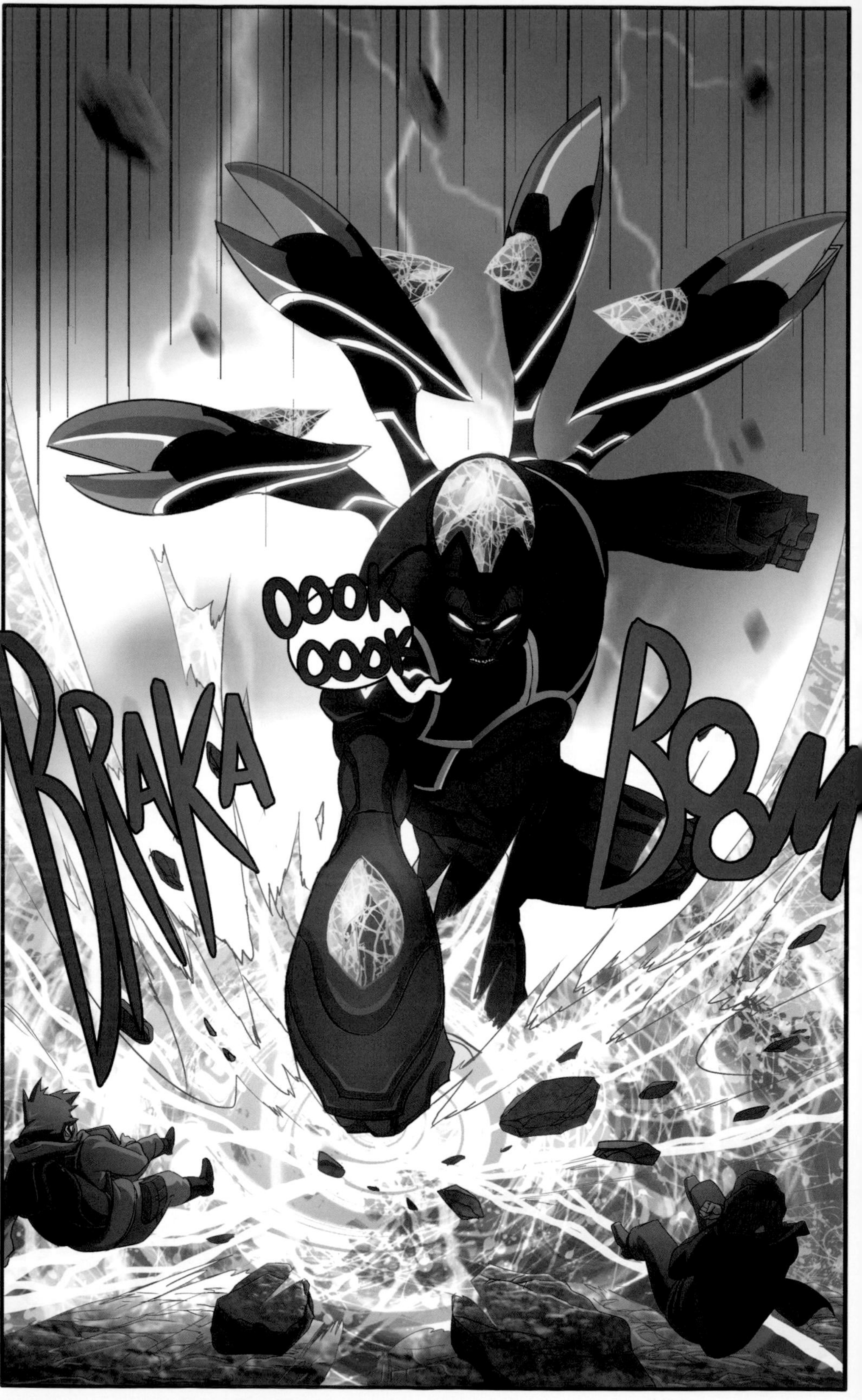
OOOK
OOOK
BRAKA
BOOM

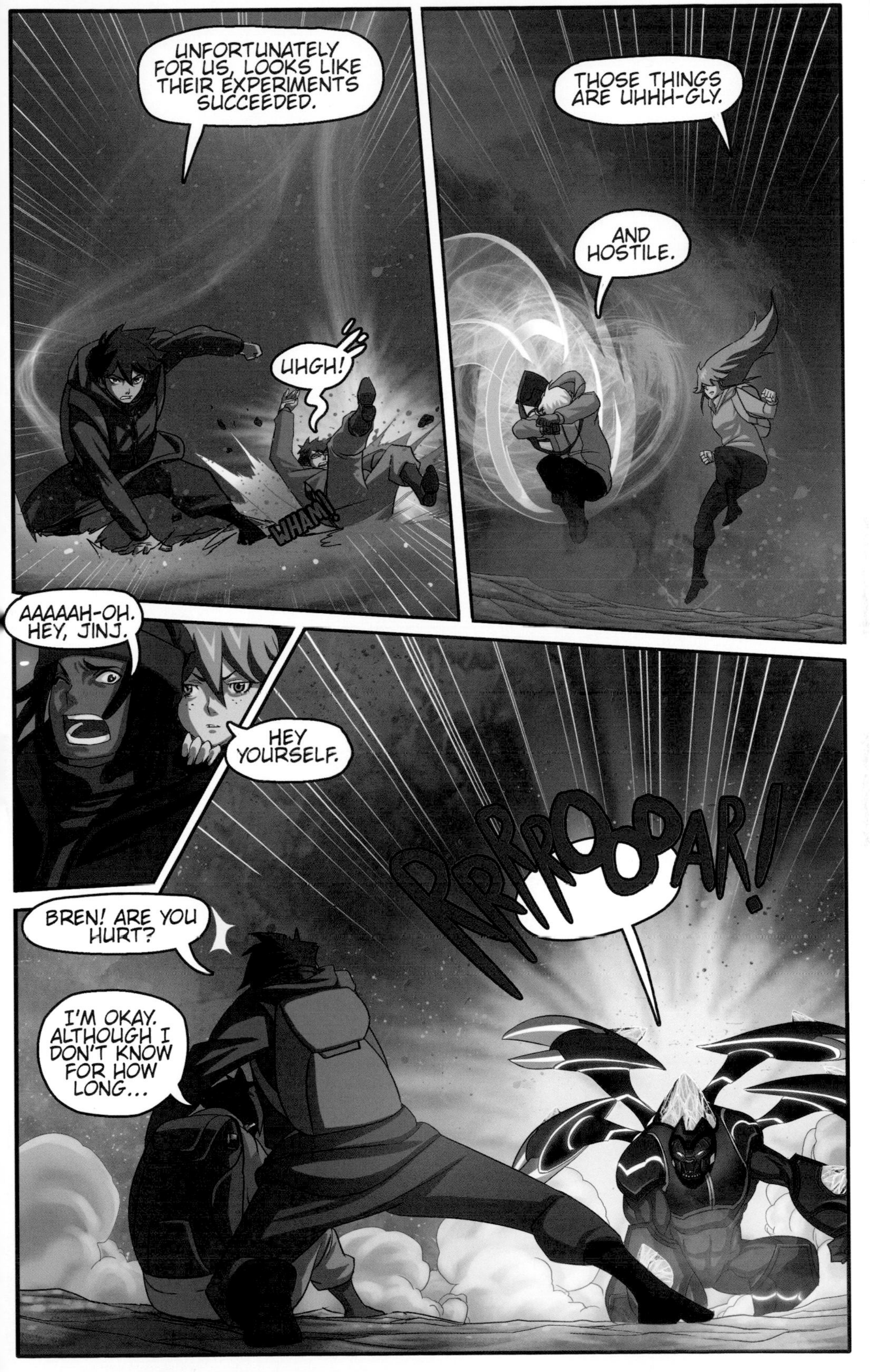

UNFORTUNATELY FOR US, LOOKS LIKE THEIR EXPERIMENTS SUCCEEDED.
UHGH!
WHAM!
THOSE THINGS ARE UHHH-GLY.
AND HOSTILE.
AAAAAH-OH. HEY, JINJ.
HEY YOURSELF.
RRRROOOAR!
BREN! ARE YOU HURT?
I'M OKAY. ALTHOUGH I DON'T KNOW FOR HOW LONG...

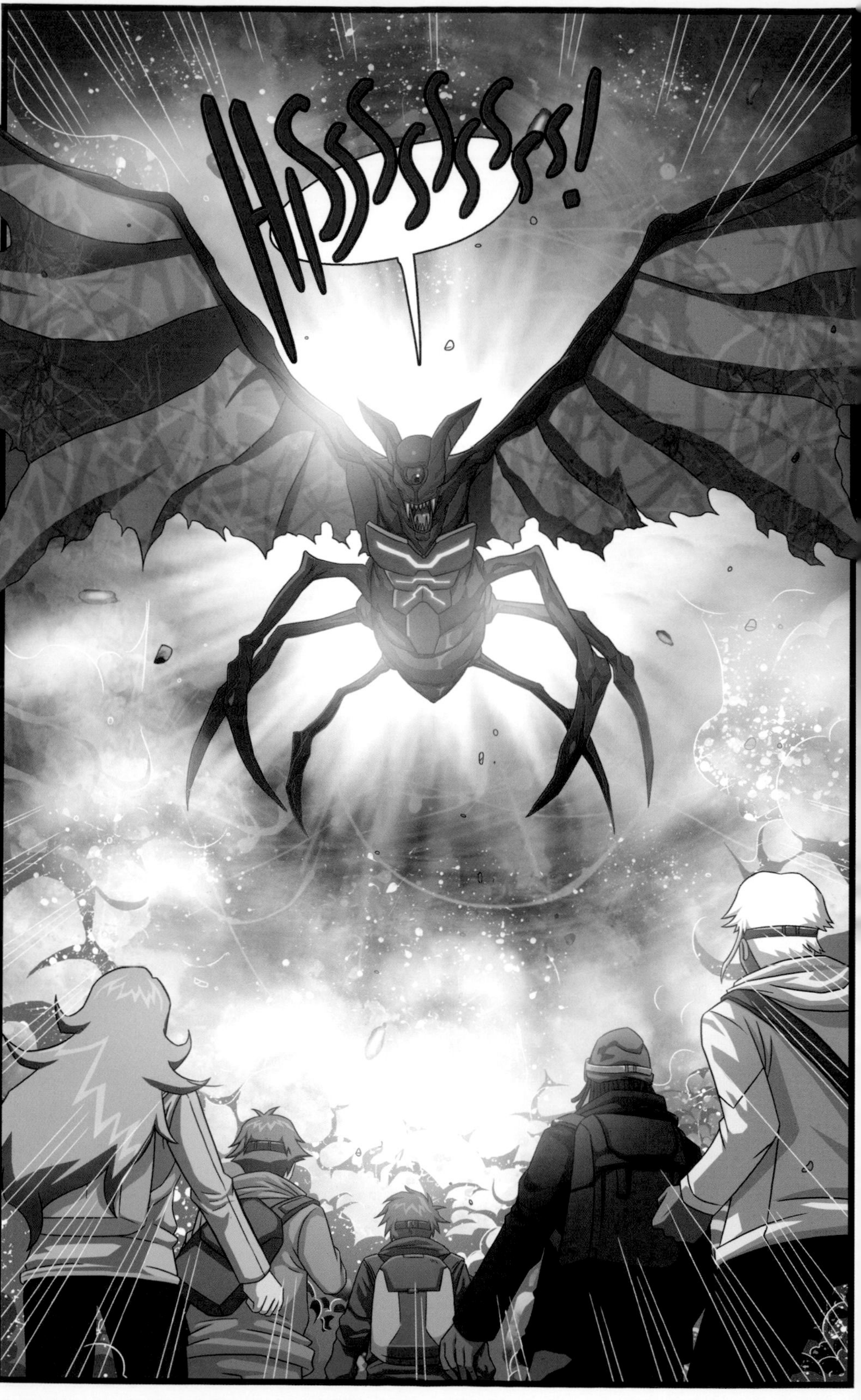
HISSSSSSSSS!

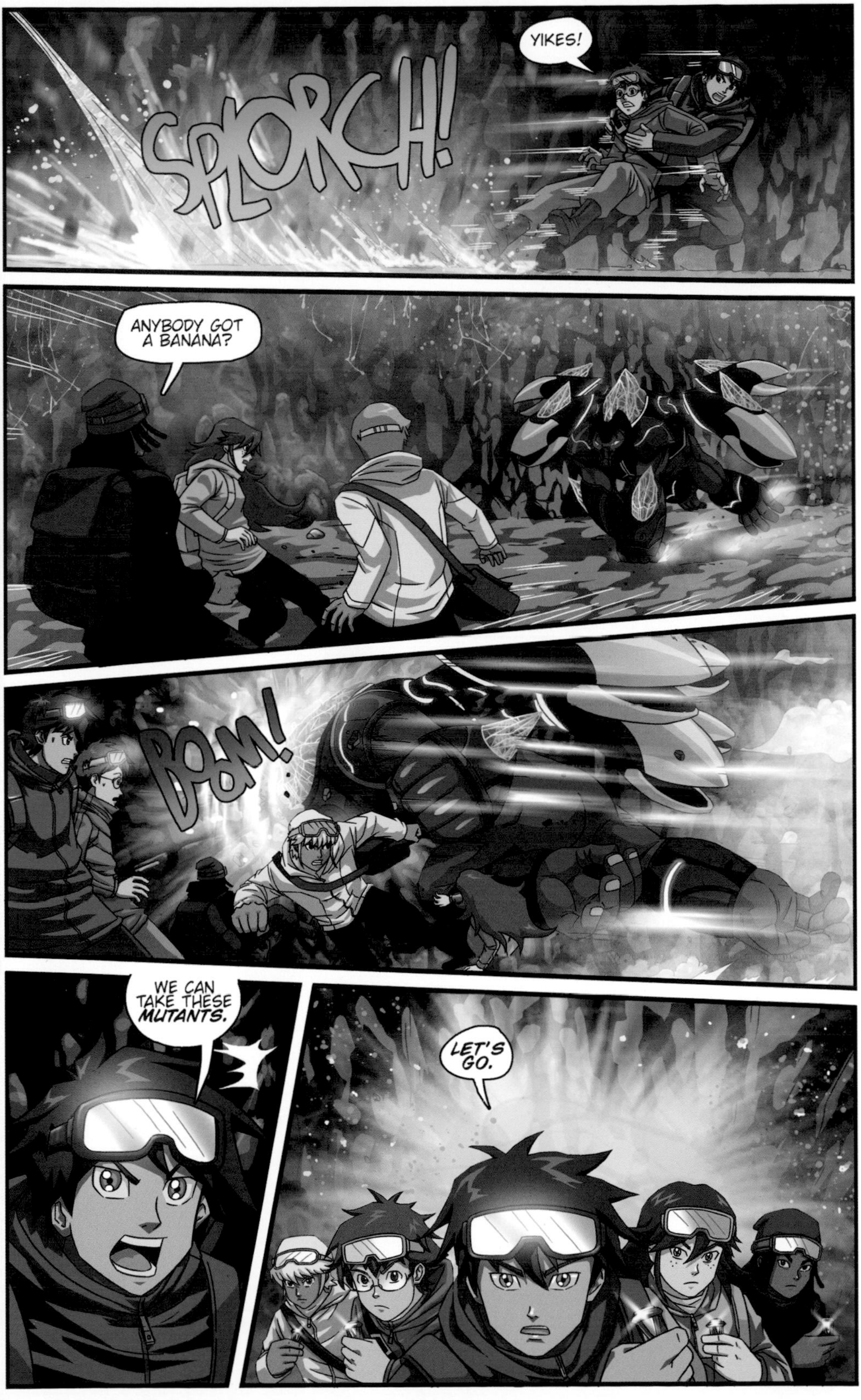
YIKES!
SPLORCH!
ANYBODY GOT A BANANA?
BOOM!
WE CAN TAKE THESE *MUTANTS.*
LET'S GO.

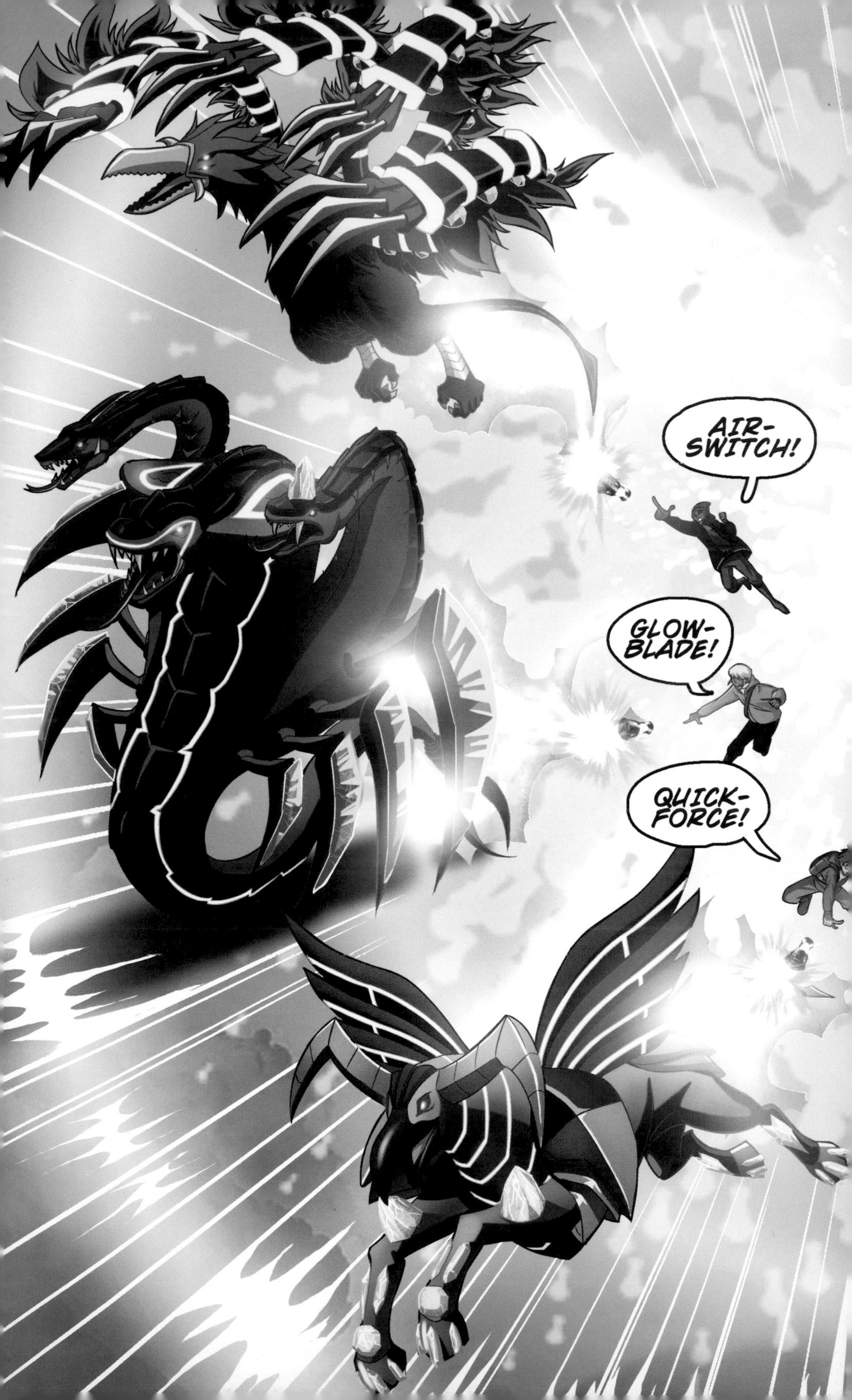
AIR-SWITCH!
GLOW-BLADE!
QUICK-FORCE!

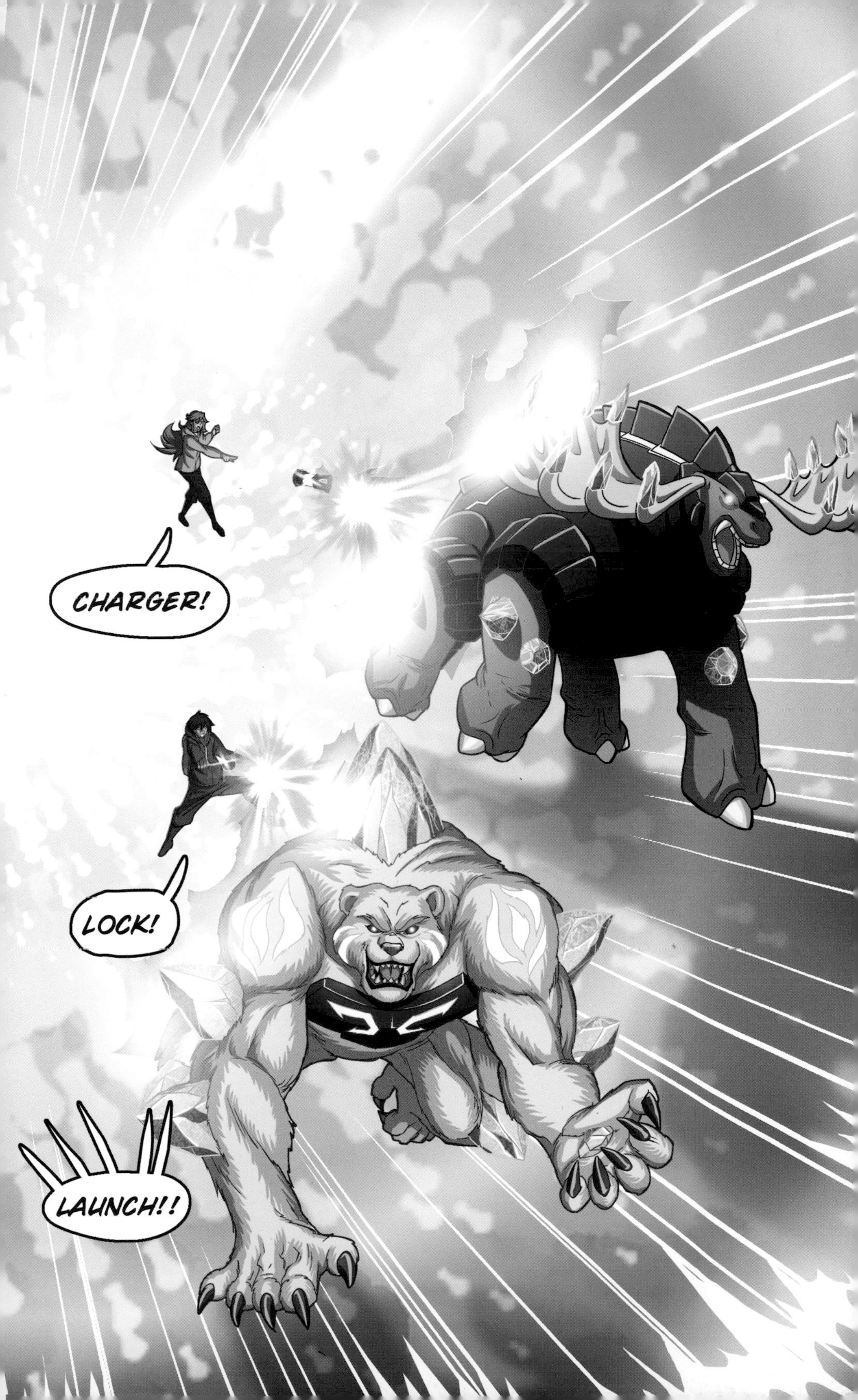
CHARGER!
LOCK!
LAUNCH!!

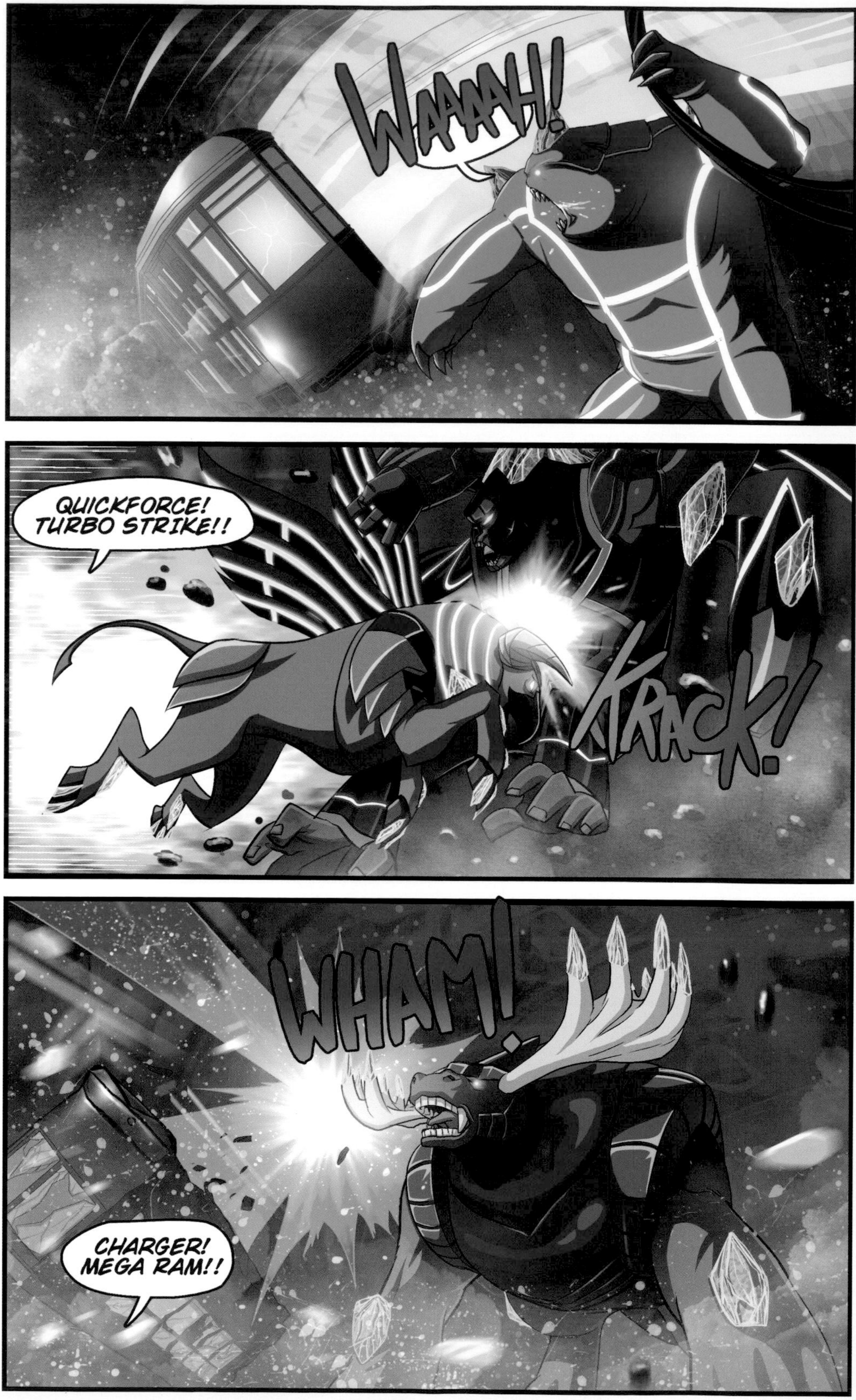
WAAAH!
QUICKFORCE! TURBO STRIKE!!
KRACK!
WHAM!
CHARGER! MEGA RAM!!

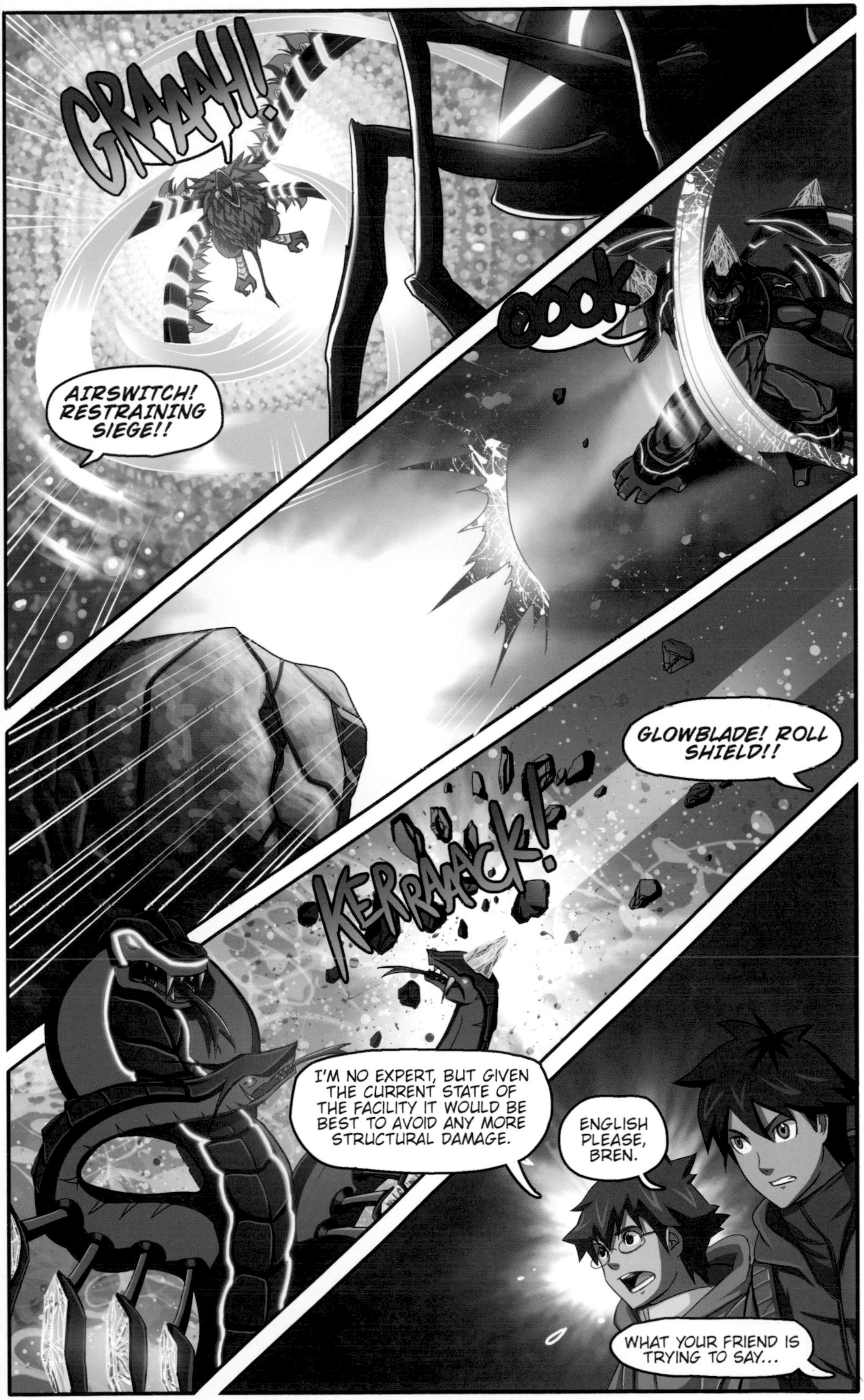
GRAAAH!
AIRSWITCH! RESTRAINING SIEGE!!
OOOK
GLOWBLADE! ROLL SHIELD!!
KERRAACK!
I'M NO EXPERT, BUT GIVEN THE CURRENT STATE OF THE FACILITY IT WOULD BE BEST TO AVOID ANY MORE STRUCTURAL DAMAGE.
ENGLISH PLEASE, BREN.
WHAT YOUR FRIEND IS TRYING TO SAY...

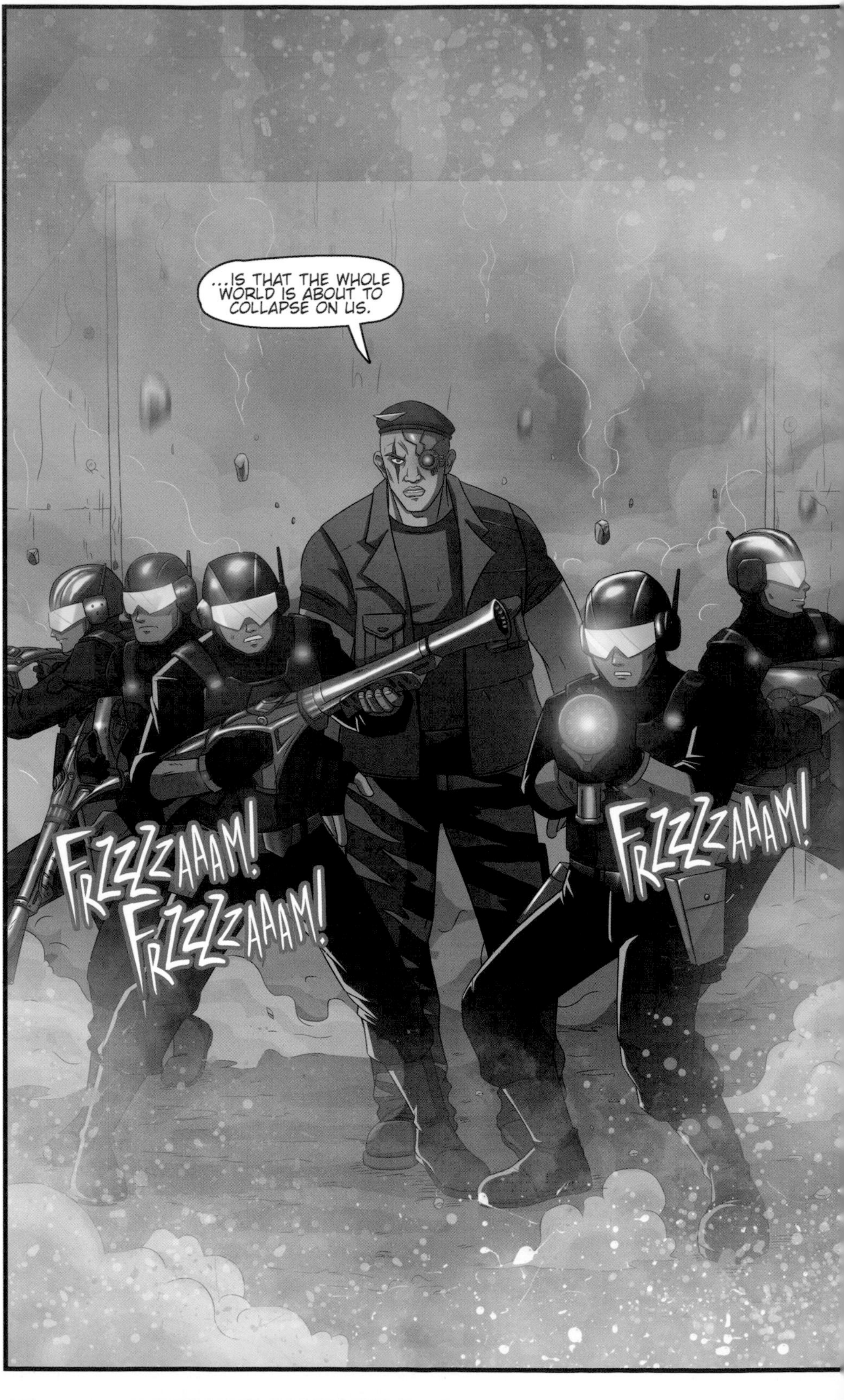
...IS THAT THE WHOLE WORLD IS ABOUT TO COLLAPSE ON US.
FRZZZZAAAM!
FRZZZZAAAM!
FRZZZZAAAM!

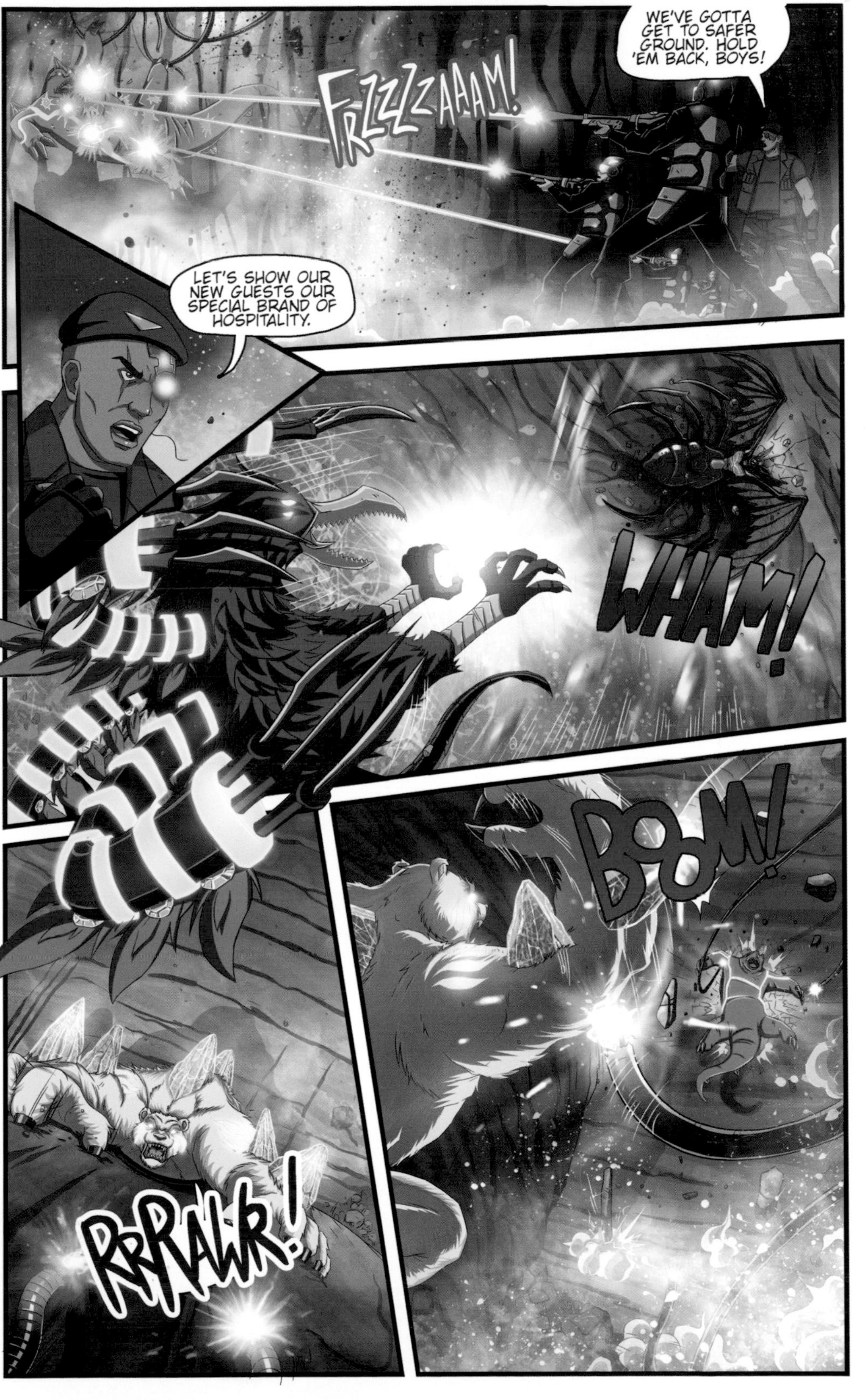
WE'VE GOTTA GET TO SAFER GROUND. HOLD 'EM BACK, BOYS!
FRZZZZAAAM!
LET'S SHOW OUR NEW GUESTS OUR SPECIAL BRAND OF HOSPITALITY.
WHAM!
BOOM!
RRRAWR!

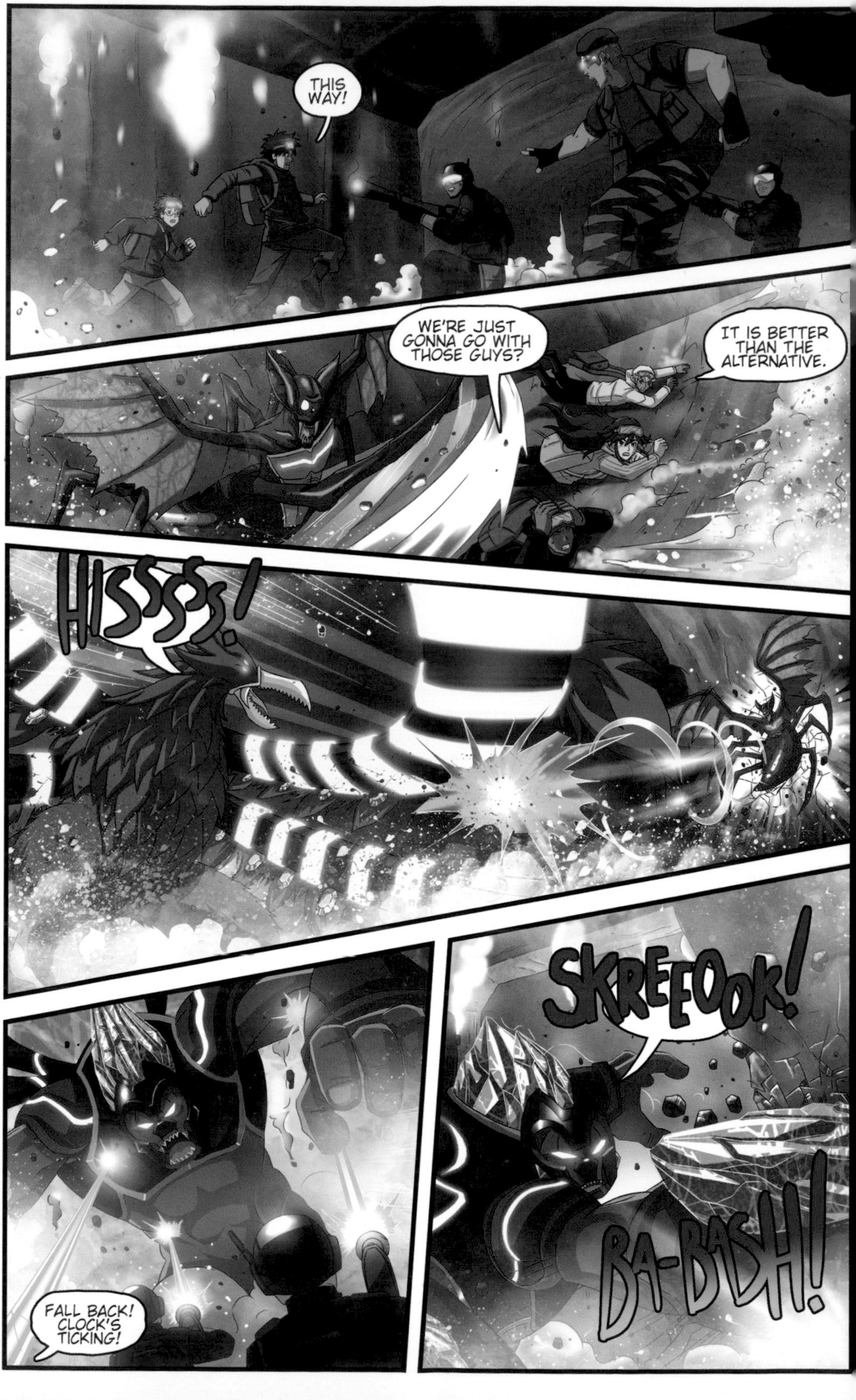
THIS WAY!
WE'RE JUST GONNA GO WITH THOSE GUYS?
IT IS BETTER THAN THE ALTERNATIVE.
HISSSSS!
SKREEOOK!
BA-BASH!
FALL BACK! CLOCK'S TICKING!

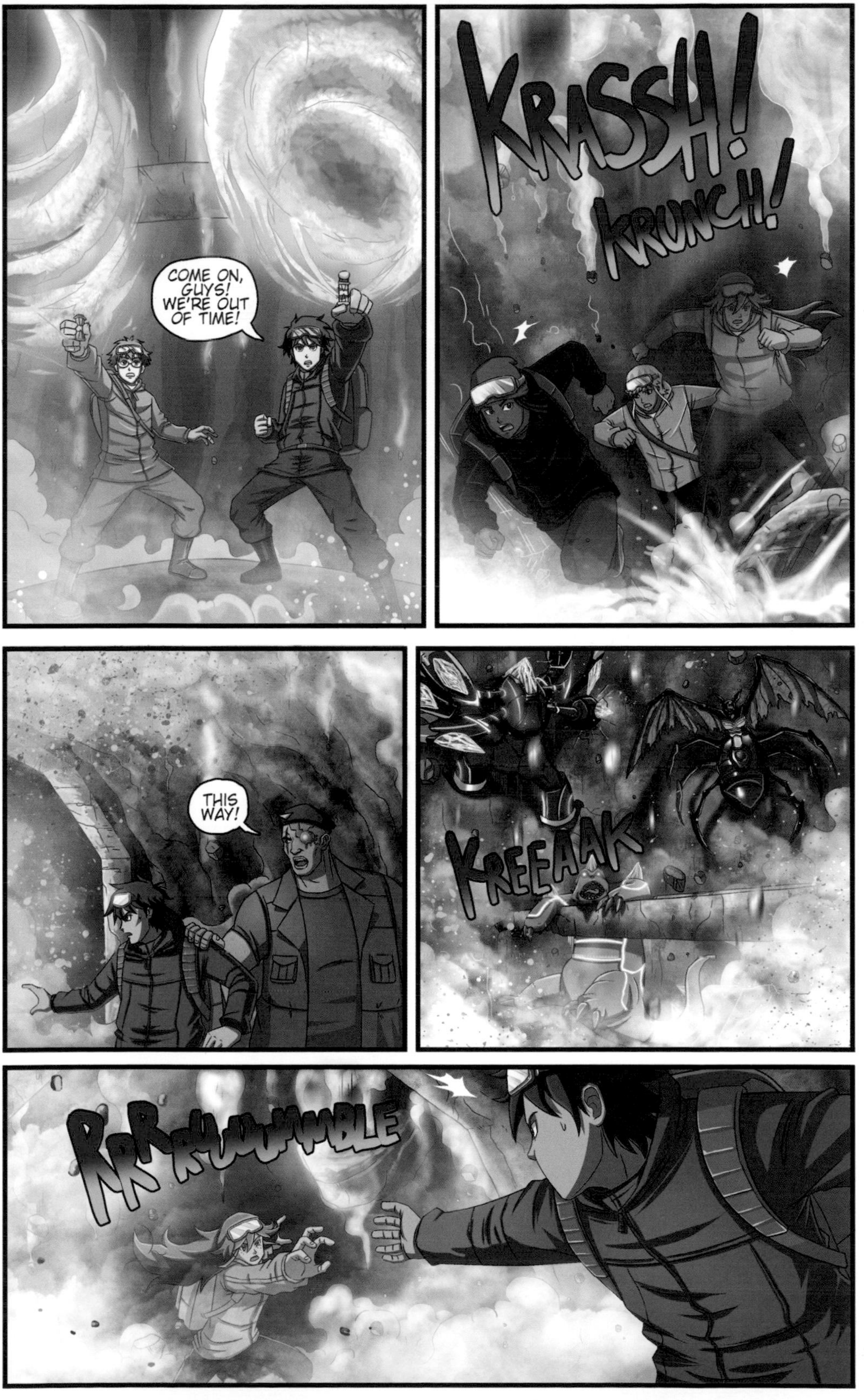
COME ON, GUYS! WE'RE OUT OF TIME!
KRASSH!
KRUNCH!
THIS WAY!
KREEAAK
RRRRUUUMMBLE

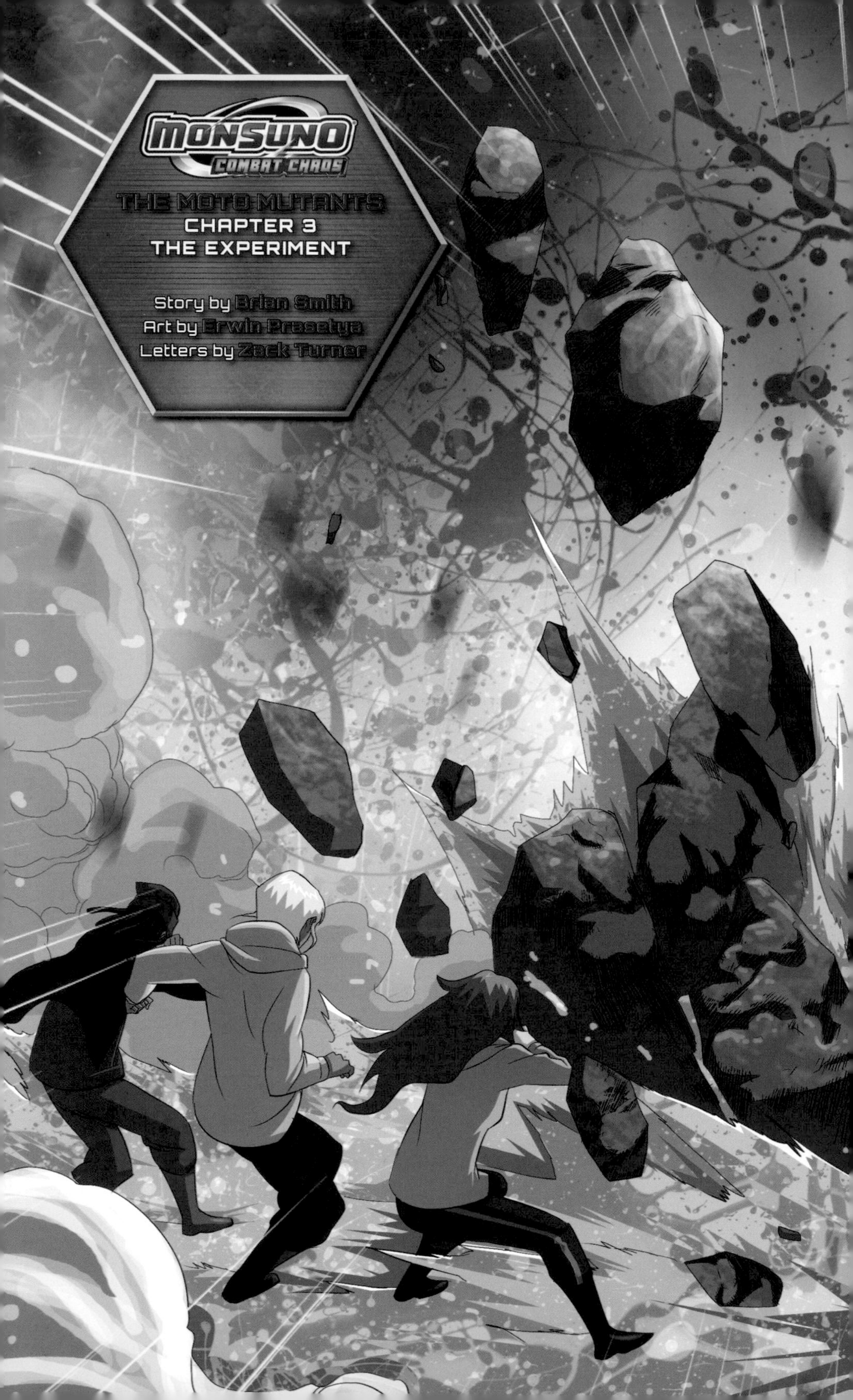
MONSUNO COMBAT CHAOS
THE MOTO MUTANTS
CHAPTER 3
THE EXPERIMENT
Story by Brian Smith
Art by Erwin Prasetya
Letters by Zack Turner

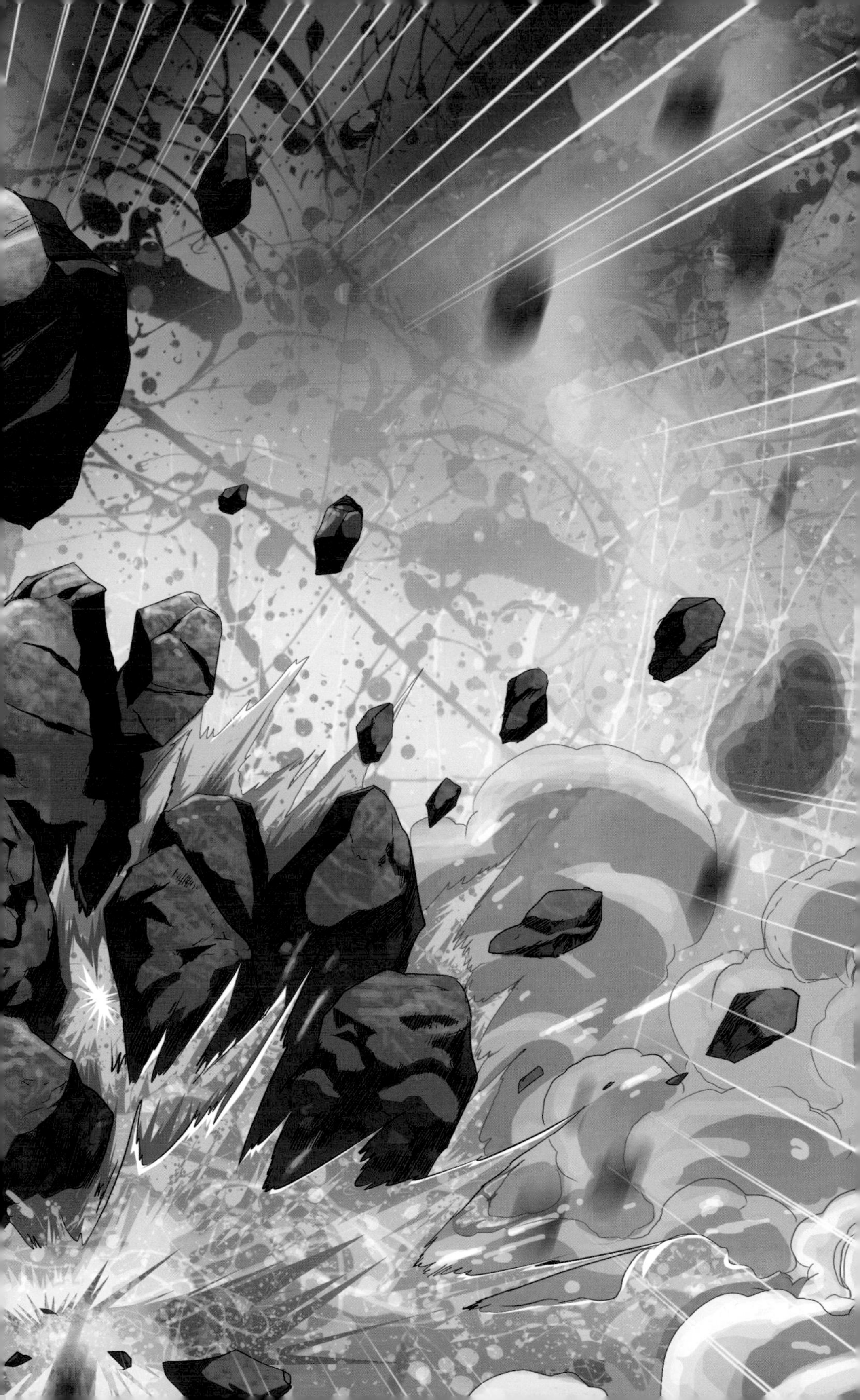

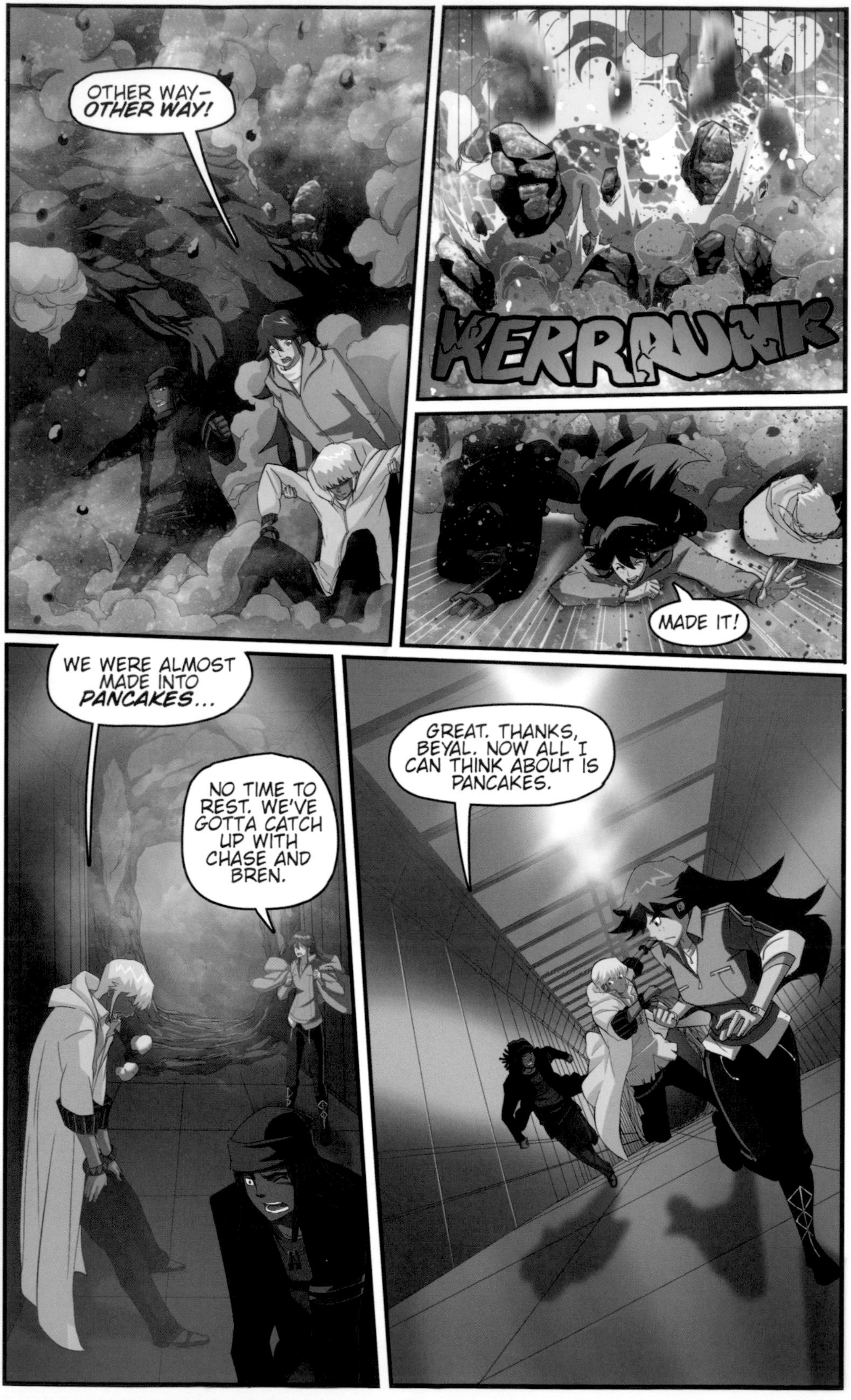
OTHER WAY—
OTHER WAY!
KERRRUNK
MADE IT!
WE WERE ALMOST MADE INTO PANCAKES...
NO TIME TO REST. WE'VE GOTTA CATCH UP WITH CHASE AND BREN.
GREAT. THANKS, BEYAL. NOW ALL I CAN THINK ABOUT IS PANCAKES.

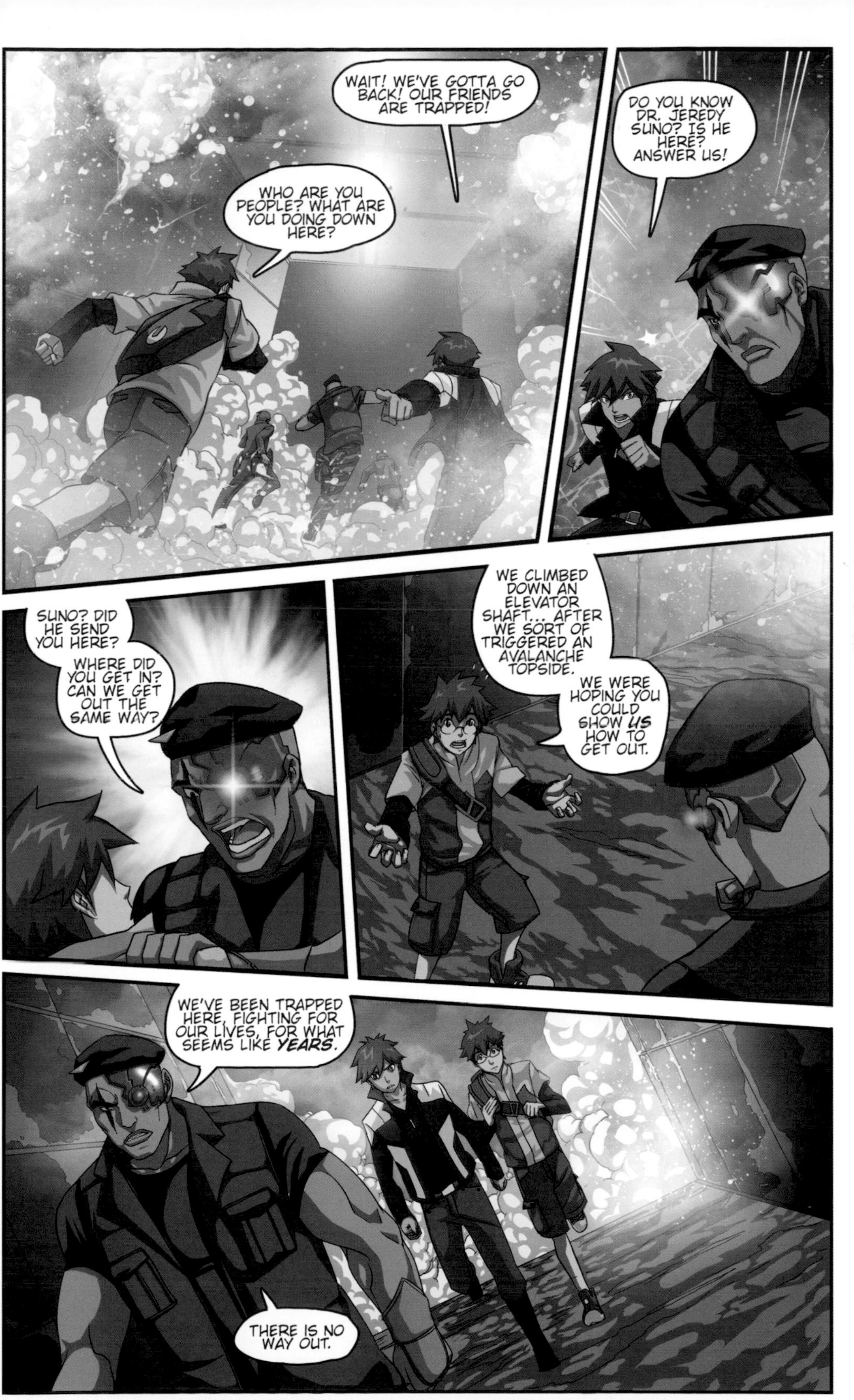
WAIT! WE'VE GOTTA GO BACK! OUR FRIENDS ARE TRAPPED!
WHO ARE YOU PEOPLE? WHAT ARE YOU DOING DOWN HERE?
DO YOU KNOW DR. JEREDY SUNO? IS HE HERE? ANSWER US!
SUNO? DID HE SEND YOU HERE?
WHERE DID YOU GET IN? CAN WE GET OUT THE SAME WAY?
WE CLIMBED DOWN AN ELEVATOR SHAFT... AFTER WE SORT OF TRIGGERED AN AVALANCHE TOPSIDE.
WE WERE HOPING YOU COULD SHOW *US* HOW TO GET OUT.
WE'VE BEEN TRAPPED HERE, FIGHTING FOR OUR LIVES, FOR WHAT SEEMS LIKE *YEARS*.
THERE IS NO WAY OUT.

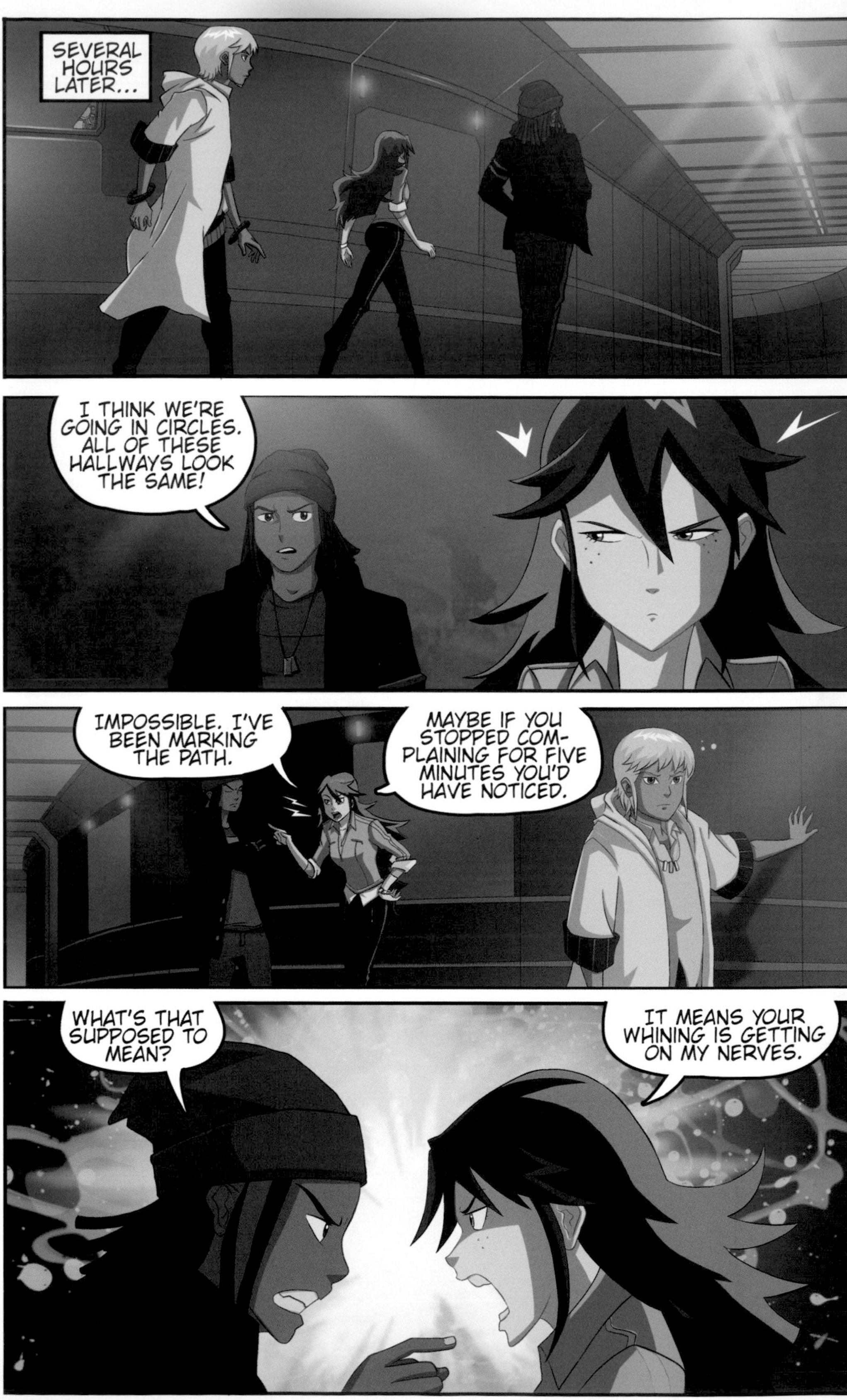
SEVERAL HOURS LATER...
I THINK WE'RE GOING IN CIRCLES. ALL OF THESE HALLWAYS LOOK THE SAME!
IMPOSSIBLE. I'VE BEEN MARKING THE PATH.
MAYBE IF YOU STOPPED COM-PLAINING FOR FIVE MINUTES YOU'D HAVE NOTICED.
WHAT'S THAT SUPPOSED TO MEAN?
IT MEANS YOUR WHINING IS GETTING ON MY NERVES.

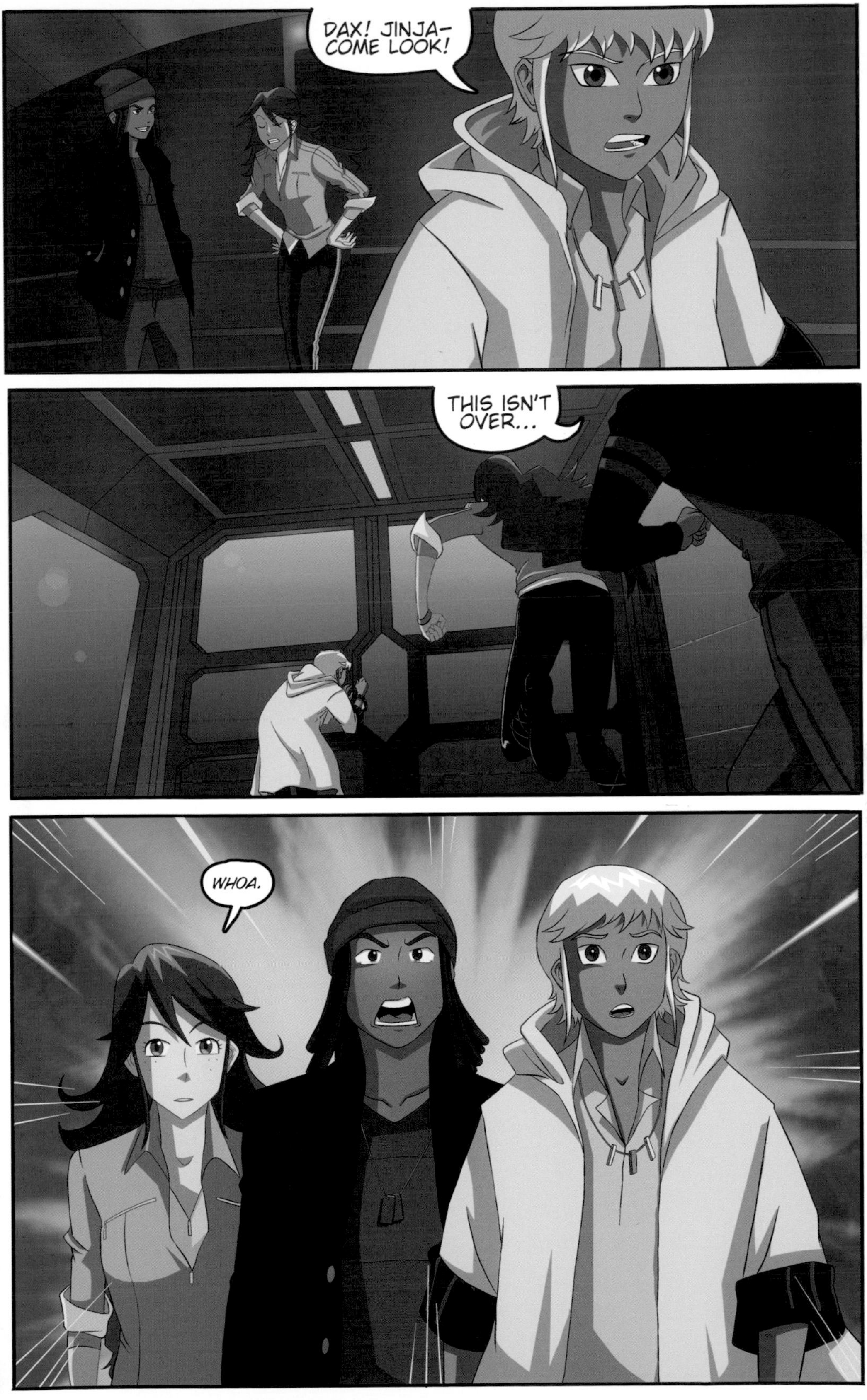
DAX! JINJA-
COME LOOK!
THIS ISN'T OVER...
WHOA.

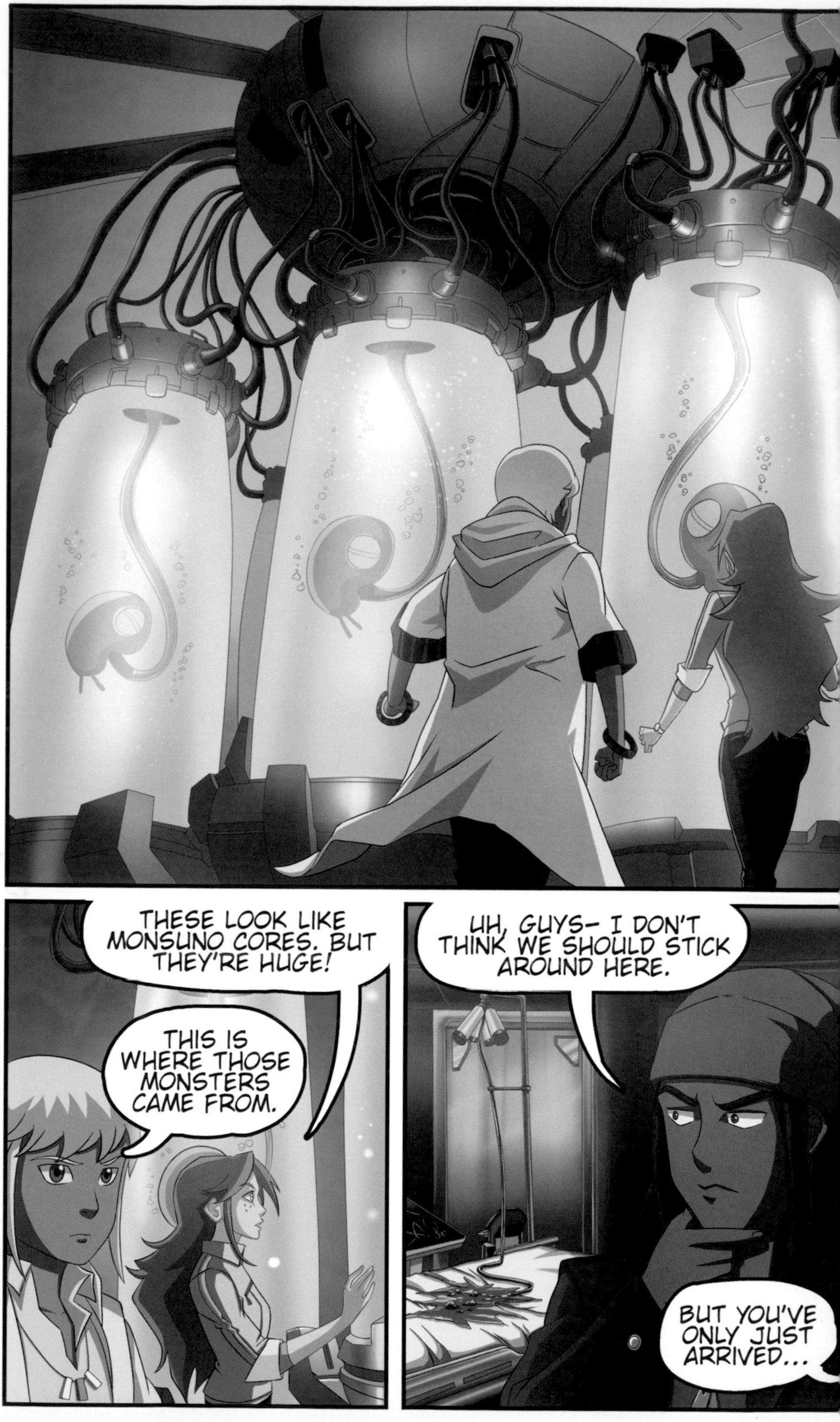
THESE LOOK LIKE MONSUNO CORES. BUT THEY'RE HUGE!
THIS IS WHERE THOSE MONSTERS CAME FROM.
UH, GUYS- I DON'T THINK WE SHOULD STICK AROUND HERE.
BUT YOU'VE ONLY JUST ARRIVED...

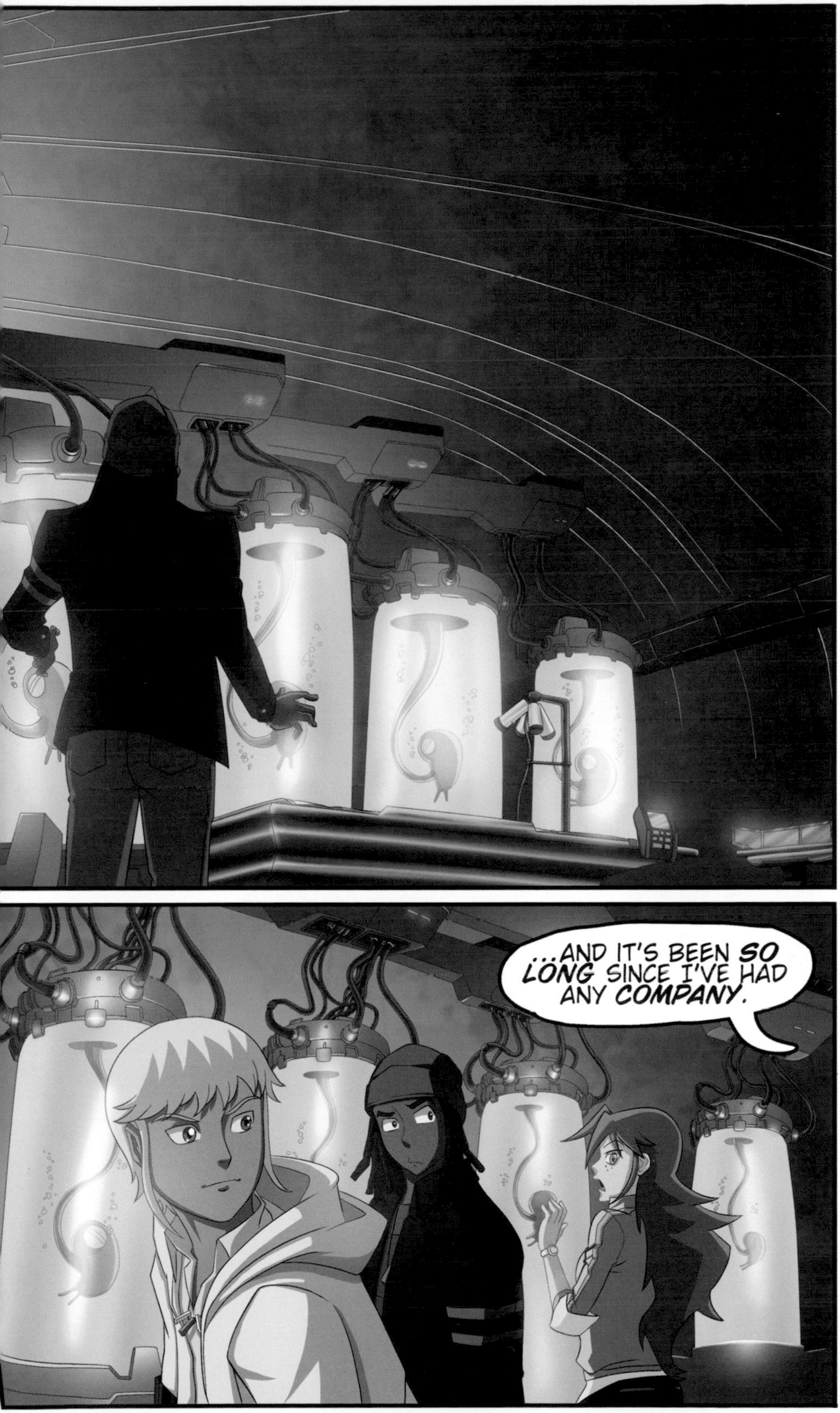
...AND IT'S BEEN SO LONG SINCE I'VE HAD ANY COMPANY.

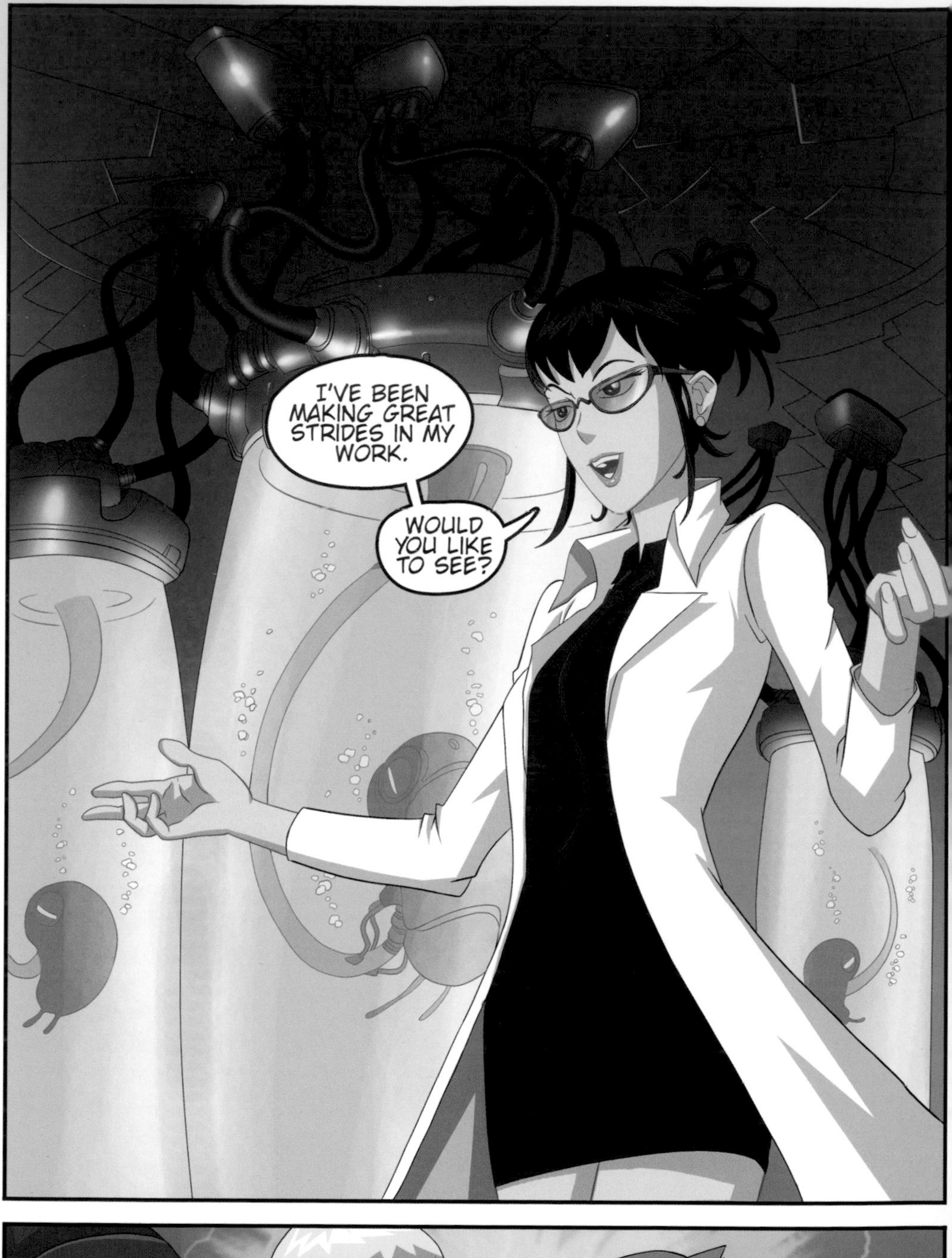
I'VE BEEN MAKING GREAT STRIDES IN MY WORK.
WOULD YOU LIKE TO SEE?
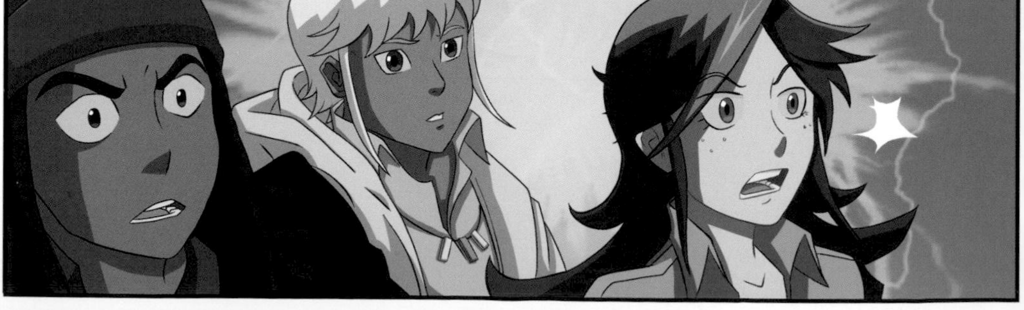

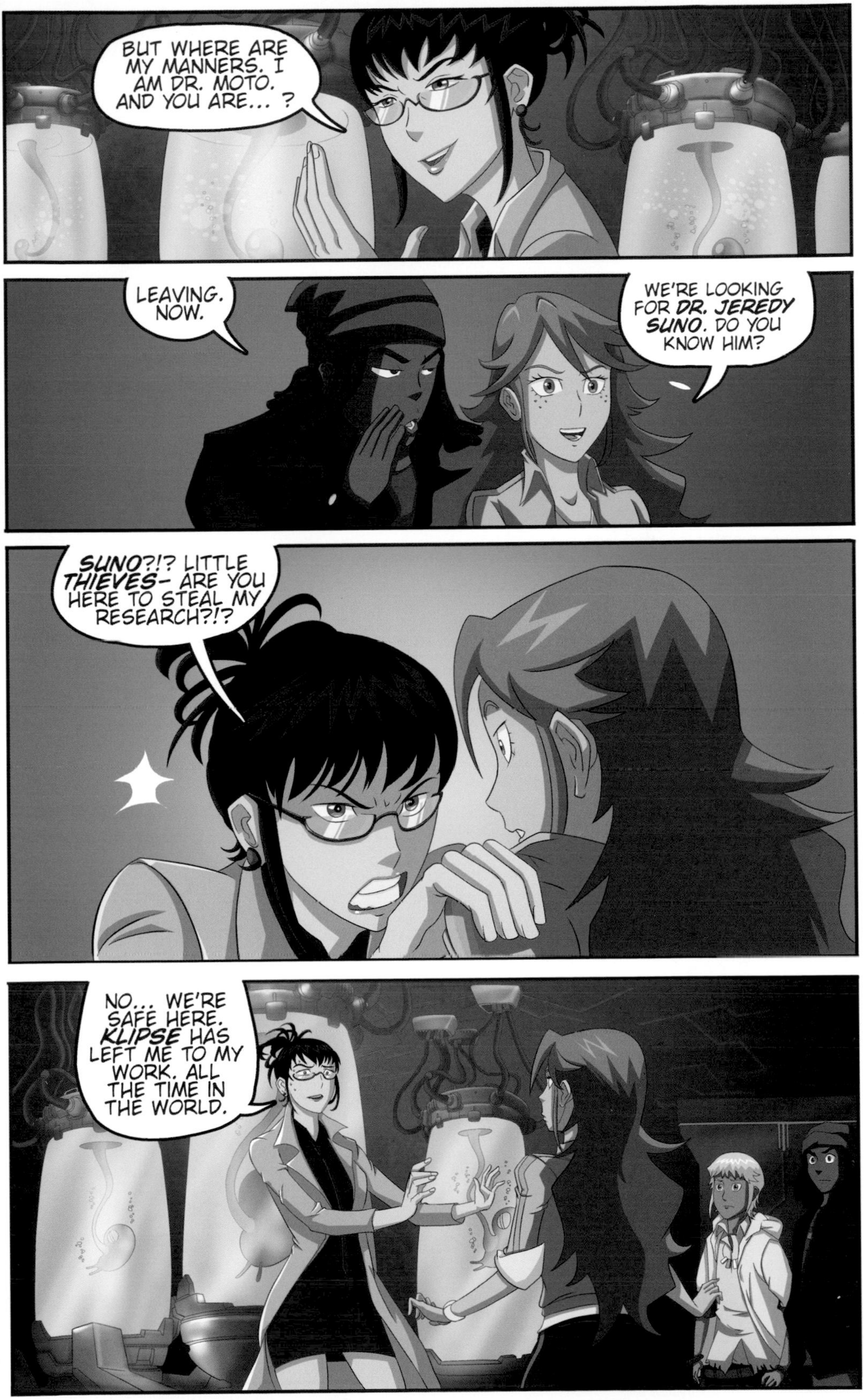
BUT WHERE ARE MY MANNERS. I AM DR. MOTO. AND YOU ARE... ?
LEAVING. NOW.
WE'RE LOOKING FOR **DR. JEREDY SUNO**. DO YOU KNOW HIM?
SUNO?!? LITTLE **THIEVES**- ARE YOU HERE TO STEAL MY RESEARCH?!?
NO... WE'RE SAFE HERE. **KLIPSE** HAS LEFT ME TO MY WORK. ALL THE TIME IN THE WORLD.

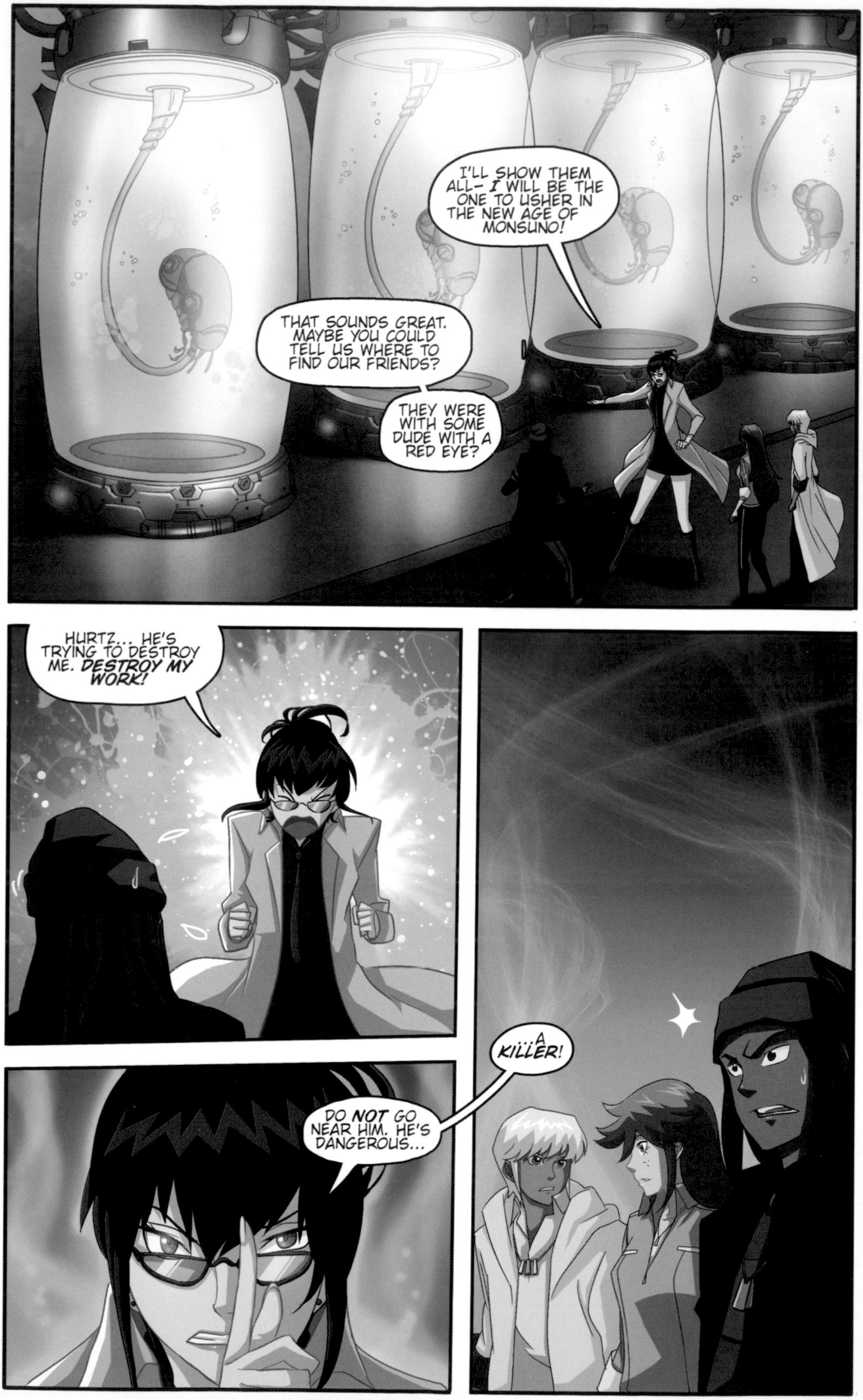
I'LL SHOW THEM ALL– I WILL BE THE ONE TO USHER IN THE NEW AGE OF MONSUNO!
THAT SOUNDS GREAT. MAYBE YOU COULD TELL US WHERE TO FIND OUR FRIENDS?
THEY WERE WITH SOME DUDE WITH A RED EYE?
HURTZ... HE'S TRYING TO DESTROY ME. DESTROY MY WORK!
DO NOT GO NEAR HIM. HE'S DANGEROUS...
...A KILLER!

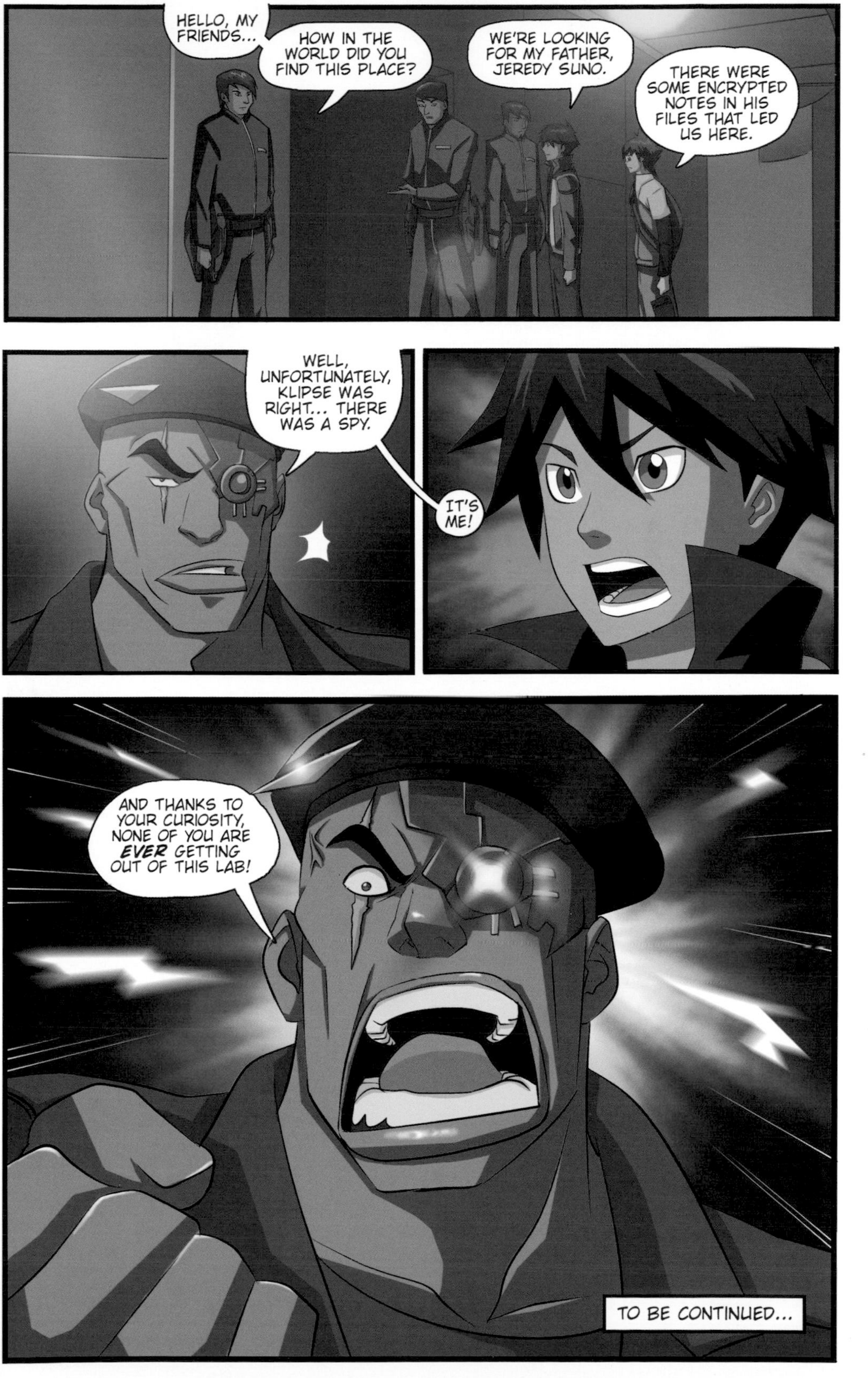
HELLO, MY FRIENDS...
HOW IN THE WORLD DID YOU FIND THIS PLACE?
WE'RE LOOKING FOR MY FATHER, JEREDY SUNO.
THERE WERE SOME ENCRYPTED NOTES IN HIS FILES THAT LED US HERE.
WELL, UNFORTUNATELY, KLIPSE WAS RIGHT... THERE WAS A SPY.
IT'S ME!
AND THANKS TO YOUR CURIOSITY, NONE OF YOU ARE ***EVER*** GETTING OUT OF THIS LAB!
TO BE CONTINUED...

WRITERS

BRIAN SMITH is a former Marvel Comics editor. His credits include *The Ultimates*, *Ultimate Spider-Man*, *Iron Man*, *Captain America*, *The Incredible Hulk*, and dozens of other comics. Smith is the co-creator/ writer behind the *New York Times* best-selling graphic novel *The Stuff of Legend*, and the writer/artist of the all-ages comic *The Intrepid EscapeGoat*. His writing credits include *Finding Nemo: Losing Dory* (BOOM!), *SpongeBob Comics* (Bongo), and *Voltron Force* (VIZ Media).

ARTISTS

PAPILLON STUDIOS

FAJAR BUANA is a colorist and illustrator for Papillon Studios who has also worked on projects for Copius Amounts Press, Supa Strike Entertainment and Arcana.

ERWIN PRASETYA is a Kudus-born artist who works for Papillon Studios and who also penciled multiple comic book series in Indonesia.

ANGGA PRASETYAWAN is a freelance penciler and illustrator with Papillon Studios. He has been drawing his own comics since he was in elementary school.

ALFA ROBBI was born and raised in Semarang City, Central Java, Indonesia. His published works include *Planetary Brigade* (Boom!) and *Ev* (TokyoPop). Alfa was also the illustrator for *Voltron Force: Rise of the Beast King* (VIZ Media). Robbi's current focus is Papillon, a comic book art studio he founded with Fajar Buana in 2002.

ARUM SETIADI is a freelance inker with Papillon Studios who has also worked as a penciler for various publishers and magazines. He's a massive comics fan and started drawing after watching the anime *Dragon Ball*!

FANDHI GILANG WIJANARKO is an inker and colorist with Papillon Studios. He also recently inked *Voltron Force: Rise of the Beast King* (VIZ Media).

LETTERER

ZACK TURNER started out in the comics industry as an independent artist and colorist who worked on *Unimaginable* (Arcana) and several projects for Bluewater. Recently he has been working on full art duties on *Redakai* (VIZ Media).

BONUS SKETCHES

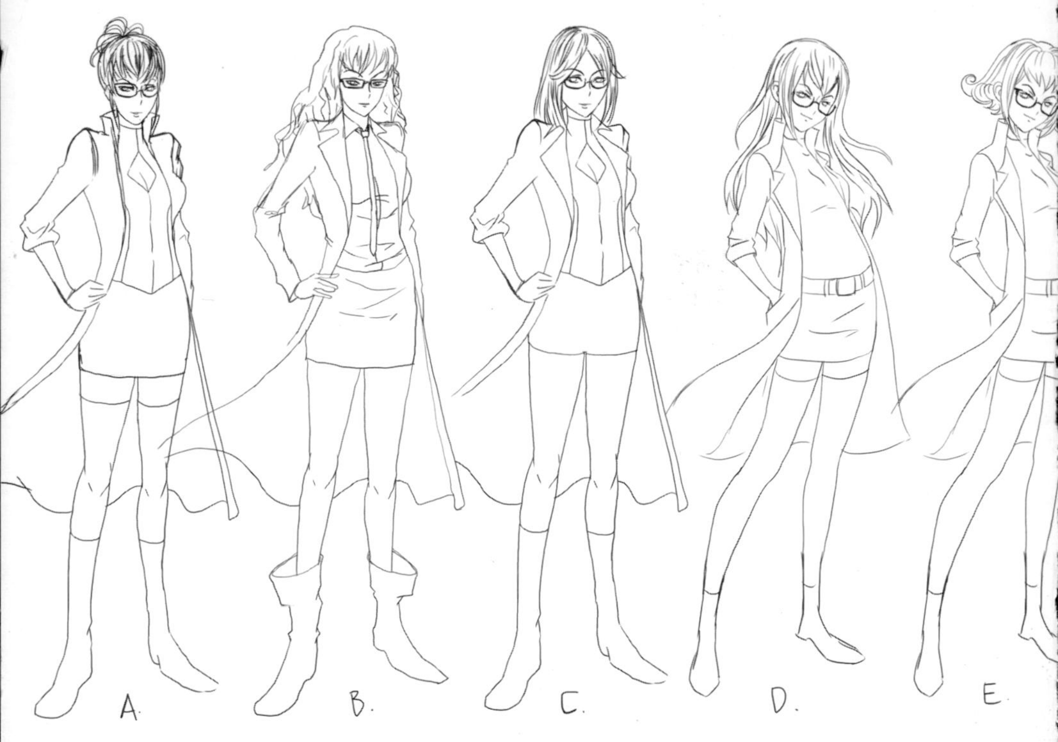
A.
B.
C.
D.
E.

Early Dr. Moto Designs by Alfa Robbi